HILL MAN

Other books by Janice Holt Giles
published by The University Press of Kentucky

The Believers

The Enduring Hills

40 Acres and No Mule

Hannah Fowler

The Kentuckians

The Land Beyond the Mountains

Miss Willie

The Plum Thicket

HILL MAN

Janice Holt Giles

With a Foreword by Wade Hall

THE UNIVERSITY PRESS OF KENTUCKY

Publication of this volume was made possible in part by grants from
the E.O. Robinson Mountain Fund
and the National Endowment for the Humanities.

Editorial and Sales Offices: The University Press of Kentucky
663 South Limestone Street, Lexington, Kentucky 40508-4008

04 03 02 01 00   5 4 3 2 1

Library of Congress Cataloging-in-Publication Data

Giles, Janice Holt.
    Hill man / Janice Holt Giles.
        p. cm.
    "Published in 1954 by Pyramid Books of New York under the
    pen name of John Garth"—P. 1.
    ISBN 0-8131-2165-5 (alk. paper)
        1. Mountain life—Kentucky—Fiction. 2. Farm life—Kentucky
    —Fiction. 3. Kentucky—Fiction. I. Title.

PS3513.I4628 H55 2000
813'.54—dc21   99-055677

Foreword

Wade Hall

In October of 1945, when Janice Holt married Henry Giles in Louisville just after he returned from service in World War II, she acquired not only a husband but considerable literary property. It was his home community of Giles Ridge in Adair County in south central Kentucky, an area whose rich history and culture she would mine for her books the rest of her life. After four years in Louisville, she moved with Henry to a forty-acre farm on Giles Ridge, an area where she and Henry would live until her death in 1979 and his death in 1986.

Before the move Janice had already written two novels, *The Enduring Hills* and *Miss Willie.* By 1954, with Henry's help, she had written and published six more books, all, with the exception of *The Kentuckians,* set in her adopted community. *Hill Man* was one of those books.

Called "Vengeance" in manuscript, *Hill Man* was written in 1951, just after Janice had completed *40 Acres and No Mule,* an autobiographical account of their life in the hill country. Three years later, in 1954, *Hill Man* was finally published. Her first three novels had been published under the somewhat confining editorial policies of Westminster Press, a Presbyterian publishing house; *Harbin's Ridge* and *Hill Man* were the first two manuscripts submitted to her new publisher, Houghton Mifflin, by her agent, Oliver Swan. *Harbin's Ridge* was immediately accepted, but *Hill Man* was declined. Swan also offered the manuscript to Harcourt Brace and Harper and Brothers, but no one would take it, calling it formless, too episodic, and centered around an unattractive character. Then she authorized Swan to submit it to a paperback publisher under a pseudonym, and so *Hill Man* was finally published in 1954 by Pyramid Books of New York under the pen name of John Garth, with a first printing of 300,000 copies. It would be her only original paperback book.

The fact is that *Hill Man* was a radical departure from her earlier novels that had built for her an image and a large readership. Apparently chafing under the constrictions and revisions required by Westminster, she had told Oliver Swan that it had been "a great joy to turn with freedom and a sense of integrity" to *Harbin's Ridge* and *Hill Man*. Although *Hill Man* became a kind of orphaned book, it was one that she valued for its earthiness and accuracy. After reading the galley proofs for the book, she wrote the publisher: "I was struck by its strength. It is the most realistic ridge book we have written, completely honest and presenting the truest picture of most of the ridge men." Furthermore, despite his amorality, she considered her protagonist, Rady Cromwell, "thoroughly likeable" for his "unwillingness to be beaten." Elsewhere she said, "Rady is not fiction. He is fact."

In fact, however, Rady Cromwell is a backwoods hero and sexual athlete most of her readers were not prepared to accept. Set on Bruton Ridge, *Hill Man* presented another view of the hill life Janice had portrayed with a certain romantic aura and delicacy in *Miss Willie* and *Tara's Healing*. Many readers and critics had already noted the "masculine strength" of Janice's writing, but without the puritanical and marketing restraints of church and mainline publishers she was free to write a more comprehensive, honest picture of hill life that included frank treatments of sexuality.

Giles asked the publisher not to use a "lurid cover"; nevertheless, the cover of the 25-cent paperback edition of *Hill Man* showed a shirtless young farmer at his plow eyeing a sophisticated-looking young woman with a mixture of puzzlement and attraction. Above the title a teaser labeled the contents "The earthy story of a Kentucky mountaineer and a city woman." The real identity of John Garth was revealed soon after the book's publication.

Although the novel is fleshed-out with a gallery of colorful characters, the story belongs first and foremost to Rady Cromwell, the son of a country Baptist preacher. By the time he has reached sixteen, however, he has rejected his father's moral strictures and has learned to shoot craps, play stud poker, drink moonshine, and make all manner of mischief. At twelve he was able to turn an ordinary hollow reed into a "touch-off," a homemade gun that he used to win a turkey shoot. Before he is a grown man he has become a shrewd prankster, hell-raiser, and con man with an ability to separate people from their money and land. He is also a bold, crafty, hard-working, good-natured, inventive, exciting young man possessed with muscular good looks. For his daring and dangerous ways, he is admired by men and loved by women. He is a charming backwoods promoter and entrepreneur who pulls himself up the social and economic ladder, step by step, until he has mastered and used any number of women, including two wives. He is always the opportunist in the business of "bettering himself." His other talents include playing his guitar and singing "song-ballats" like "Lord Thomas" and "Barby Allen."

Rady always gets what he wants: first a gun, then a dog and a guitar. Then he wanted a widow and her farm. Then he wanted an even more beautiful widow and her property. As his admiring narrator says, "He didn't know yet how he would get them, but he never doubted for a minute that he would. For besides it being his nature to want certain things, it was his nature also to get what he wanted."

Rady's robust libido is easily satisfied without moral qualms. His awareness of his own sexuality is described by Giles's narrator: "Rady looked at his own body, curved smooth and hard, and like copper in the firelight, his legs ropey and tough with young muscles. . . . Clean and young and unbending strong. Like a bobcat, crouched to spring, ready to rip. Wound up and tight-sprung, he was about to burst with the good way he felt, and he stretched long and touched the foot of the bed with his toes." Women who fall deeply, hopelessly in love with him are easy prey. He watches helplessly as his first wife is being gored by a raging bull, and "it flashed into and across his mind that with Annie gone nothing but Mister Rowe stood between him and that fine farm, and Mister Rowe was a sick man. With Annie gone he'd still have all he'd ever had with her, and he'd be free to get the rest." Despite his admiration for Rady, the narrator also has sympathy for the women he victimizes: "It's a sad thing," he says, "but when a woman lets a man have his way with her she gives him the upper hand every time. She hands over to him the best that she's got, expecting him to cherish it, and he don't."

During a protracted seduction episode he admits to his love object that "I ain't a pertickler nice feller." Indeed, only a master writer could have created such an attractive, alluring rogue. Only the hand of a master writer like Giles could have described in such poignant detail the love longing of the starved and hungry Cordelia Rowe, who is powerless in the face of the sexual magnetism of her hired farm manager. Only a major talent could have gone to such depths to dissect the psychology of their doomed relationship. Only an artist could have painted the sylvan seduction scene, adulterous though it is, without pruriency or primness: "Like a water-dry deer, they slaked the long thirst of their mouths, drinking deep and greedy, until neither of them had any breath left. Like starved pieces of living flesh seeking food, their hands and their mouths looked for and found the places of love, neither of them saying a word, neither of them even knowing when they sank down to the bed of moss on the bank of the brook." In following his nature he eventually destroys the women who love him. "Just by being yourself," his second wife finally accuses him, "you hurt!" Despite his faults, however, Rady Cromwell is one of the strongest, most believable, and memorable backwoods characters in recent American fiction. Moreover, in his daring and relentless pursuit of his ambition, he achieves tragic stature.

The story of *Hill Man* is Rady's story, but he does not tell it. It is told by an unnamed observer-narrator who participates in and chronicles his friend's rise and fall. In fact, he reconstructs

Rady Cromwell's life not only from personal observation but more importantly from his imagination. In recording the gory details of the gruesome death of Rady's first wife, he writes: "Rady never had to say much for me to see the whole thing just like it happened." He is an uncommonly articulate narrator, a composite, one assumes, of both Janice and Henry Giles that explains the feminine and masculine sensibilities inherent in his narrative.

In describing Rady's lust for land, he writes: "There's nothing like reaching down and picking up a handful of the earth, crumbling it between your fingers, smelling it and even tasting it and knowing it's your own. This little patch of dirt, weedy, scrubby, even rocky, is what's yours of the whole wide world. You can stand strong on it because it belongs to you." Once, when the narrator states a sentiment sympathetic to women, he quickly inserts a disclaimer: "I misdoubt there ever was a woman didn't feel a kind of sin with a man. Even when it's a nice, legal sin. Or maybe it's the sin makes it nice. Not being a woman, I wouldn't know. But I've thought on it."

For his part, the narrator revels in the free and wild life that he had enjoyed with Rady when they were boys: "Take a young feller, green and full of his own juices, and make him healthy and untwisted and unsoured, and you got about as fine a being as the Lord ever created . . . perfect, that is, for his own uses and his own purposes, in his own time and place." In fact, he never judges Rady, even when he realizes the probability that Rady has fathered his own wife's first child or when he is seduced into a moonshining operation with Rady that results in a murder and prison sentence. More than likely, he will praise Rady's boyish pranks and manly aberrations as well as his self-assured skills: "Like everything else he did, Rady did a nice job plowing."

As Janice has noted, however, it is the narrator who is the typical hill man, a man who lacks a lot of ambition and would rather hunt or fish than plow his cornfield. Furthermore, he is a man who doesn't take big risks. That is why he is the anonymous narrator, and the hero of the story he tells is the ambitious, wily, hard-working Rady. Although a tragic hero with serious flaws,

Rady also has his good points. The narrator asserts that Rady did his duty by sitting up with his wife's corpse all night long and "never once closed his eyes." And finally Rady accepts major responsibility for an illegal distillery and fatal shoot-out and serves time in prison. And most importantly, after he's lost everything, when he is "right back down to scratch," he refuses to give up. "He never quit trying. Like a bulldog hanging on, he kept trying." It is this dogged spirit that triumphs in the end.

Although *Hill Man* is one of Giles's early novels, by the time she wrote it she had already mastered the speech and folkways of Henry's hill people and uses them convincingly and without condescension in this novel. Here is a veritable folk community revealed, a cultural backwater that is like a living museum showing life as it was lived a century and more ago. From tobacco raising and moonshining to a game of skill called the turkey shoot, here is a community where the people speak an archaic English with "hit" for "it," "twicet" for "twice," and "meeting" for "church," where a woman is "proud-chested" and a man does "a mort of work" and the official witnesses at a wedding are said "to stand up" at the ceremony. It is a society where entertainment is home-made, and practical jokes—like running a mule through a camp meeting to break it up—are straight out of the antebellum humor of the Old Southwest. It is a community where a bride and groom can expect to be embarrassed and kept from going to bed on their wedding night by a noisy "shivaree."

It is also a society in which men are men and do manly things and women are women and do feminine things. A man's world is filled with hard work and occasional bouts of excusable drinking, carousing, hunting and fishing, and marital infidelity. And the women are expected to understand their men's ways and welcome them back when they return from their holidays. The men take their pleasure from their women, but they generally prefer to be with each other.

This novel celebrates the ridge culture of male camaraderie, in particular, when Rady, Jim Crowe, and the narrator go foxhunting one night, "free and unhampered," leaving family and work and worries behind: "A free man, for a time, a free and new-young and sapling-strong man. With a fire burning bright and you squatted in front of it, and a jug to tilt, the likker hot and good inside you, the dogs yipping off somewheres in the dark, the stars so close the tops of the trees are brushed with them. Man, it's good!" To top it off, Rady plays his guitar and sings. As the narrator comments: "A woman don't never seem to understand a man's need to bust loose once in a while. Women don't seem to have the need. Or if they do they take it out in scrubbing the floors or washing the quilts or putting new paper on the walls."

Janice Holt Giles understood this male-dominated culture through and through, from the men's fondness for guns and knives to their sudden itch to go "roistering around with the boys." So does the narrator, who admits his fondness for being around Rady: "Being with him always made me feel good." Everyone takes it for granted that married men will sometimes stray from their wives. Rady is a good husband, says the narrator, but he doesn't let "a wedding ceremony put an end to his natural pleasures."

Despite its setting in the mid-1920s and its authorship in the 1950s, *Hill Man* is a contemporary novel, with the timeless themes and patterns and the elemental starkness of a Greek trag-edy. This raw and realistic portrayal of hill life is one of Giles's major achievements—and deserves to rank with Harriette Arnow's *The Dollmaker* and Elizabeth Madox Roberts's *The Time of Man* in portraying accurately and sympathetically the life of poor rural Kentuckians. No one can fully appreciate the dimen-sions of Janice Holt Giles's talent without reading *Hill Man*. It will be a welcome and tantalizing surprise for legions of Giles readers. This story, published originally as a throw-away paper-back, may indeed turn out to be one of her best. It is arguably her most honest and engrossing novel.

Unlike Rady's second wife, the ill-fated, city-bred Cordelia, who "wasn't cut out to be a ridge runner" and always remains an outsider, Janice Holt Giles managed to learn the ridge and its ways and adapt herself to them. It is Janice talking through the narrator when he says as the tragedy is ending: "I don't know how an outsider could get to know and love the ridge ways, un-less he could put behind him everything he'd ever known different, and forget there was anything more than the ridge in the world." Janice Holt Giles became a major Kentucky author and a writer of national significance by doing just that and by farming with her pen the ridges of Adair County, the priceless gift that she received as a dowry from Henry Giles.

Chapter One

There were three things Rady Cromwell loved when he was a kid. They were his old muzzle-loading rifle, his old black and tan hound dog, and his beat-up, battered old gittar. They were solid things, that he could lay his hand to, and they belonged to him. They were almost all that did belong to him, too.

The way he came by the rifle was like this. The Bruton boys over on Bruton Ridge had a turkey shoot one day in the fall. The trees were stripped already, the broom sedge was drying and crackling in the fields, the ginseng berries were turning red, and the mornings were frosted and rimed. It was coming on to Thanksgiving, the best time of year for a turkey shoot.

The Bruton boys had give out that they were having the turkey shoot, and claimed they had five turkeys to put up. Everybody was going, naturally. A turkey shoot is a big affair. Not on account of winning a turkey, for that don't amount to nothing. But on account of it giving a man a chance to show off his shooting, to brag a little, sample the moonshine, eat hearty of barbecued pig and maybe engage in a fist fight or two. In short, it was good because it was a bunch of men getting together to do the things they liked best to do.

Rady had to sneak off to go, for his old man, being a Primitive Baptist preacher, didn't hold with turkey shoots, and being a hard-working farmer as well, he wouldn't of let Rady go on account of having to spare him from work. But Rady didn't aim to let nothing keep him from going to that turkey shoot, so he got up afore day that morning, slipped out the back way and lit a shuck across the holler to Bruton Ridge. He took with him his gun. Not the rifle. He didn't have that yet. He took the one he'd made himself and it was the one he aimed to shoot in the turkey shoot.

There was to be horseshoe pitching and wrestling in the morning and then the barbecued pig. The shooting didn't come off until after dinner. But it paid a body to take the whole day, for take a bunch of hill men, each and every one as prideful and as quick to hassel as a cock rooster, likker them up a mite, let them get to bragging, and the feathers is likely to commence flying. You can always count on three or four fist fights and a knifing or two. You wouldn't want to miss none of it.

But Rady being but a little shaver yet, just bare passed twelve year old, the morning wore out kind of long for him. He was itching for the turkey shoot to commence. Not that he never liked the wrestling and the fighting. He rooted and crowed just as loud as the rest. And not that he never eat hearty of the pig. Vittles being what they were at Old Man Cromwell's, I reckon Rady enjoyed that barbecued pig better than most that tied onto it that day. But the turkey shoot was the big thing and he was honing for it to get started.

It was about one o'clock when Ed Bruton stepped out in front and raised his arm up. "All right now, men," he says, "we're gittin' ready to shoot. First turkey's up. All them aimin' on shootin', write yer names on a piece of paper an' drop it in the hat. You'll shoot as yer drawed, fifty yards, rested. Ever' man with his own piece."

The turkey was up. That is, it was tied down behind a log with just its head showing, gobbling like it knew already what was going to happen. A turkey's head at fifty yards, even rested, is pretty hard to hit. It would be a pretty good shot if it was a still target. But when you think how a turkey's head keeps weaving and moving, you can see how it takes right smart shooting to hit it. It sure takes skill.

First man drawed stepped up, stretched his Adam's apple,

licked his thumb and wet his sight, squatted and aimed. He waited until the turkey was still, then he cut loose. Missed slicker than a whistle! The crowd razzed him some and he turned red and stepped back. The next one took his place, and he missed too. Must of been ten men shoot before one of them hit the bird. He claimed it, and Ed Bruton loosed it and gave it to him. He tied the next turkey down. And the shooting went on.

I reckon it was on the third turkey that Ed drawed Rady's name. "Rady Cromwell!" he bellowed, and Rady stepped up. Ed looked at him like he didn't believe what he was seeing. "Sho', now, sonny," he says, "this ain't no time fer jokin'. Stand aside an' let a man have his time."

"I ain't jokin'," Rady says, standing his ground. "You said all that aimed to shoot put their names in the hat. I aim to shoot."

The men commenced laughing and calling out to Ed. "He's right, Ed! Wasn't nary word said about kids not takin' part. He's got you there! He's got you fair an' square, Ed!"

Ed scratched his head kind of puzzled-like. "Well, I reckon they ain't no law agin him shootin'. What you aimin' on shootin' with, sonny? Ever'body's got to shoot their own piece."

"I brung mine," and Rady reached down and picked up his gun.

Ed looked at it. "Well, I'll be a dad-blamed, egg-suckin' hound dog! Look at this here touch-off the kid's got, men! Jist take a look at it!"

And the men gathered close around to look at Rady's gun. He'd taken a reed, just a common, ordinary holler reed like grows down on the river and folks usually use for a fishing pole, and he'd wrapped it tight with sewing thread for a barrel. It must of taken him hours on end to wrap it, as neat as he'd done with no roughness or unevenness. Then he'd varnished it over good until it was smooth and pretty and stout. He'd made the stock out of walnut, cutting it all in one piece from a big chunk, then smoothing and polishing it until it was like silk. And the hammer and trigger was made of walnut too. He'd wired the barrel to the stock with real fine wire, and made it neat and stout also. He'd bored a hole for a touchhole, and for a primer he was using the head of a regular kitchen match. For a touch-off he'd driven a carpet tack into the end of the hammer. And he worked the hammer with a rubber band. It was as pretty a touch-off as any person in these parts had ever seen. The men handled it and sighted it and talked. "How fur'll it shoot, kid?" they asked.

"I kin hit that turkey from here," Rady said.

Ed Bruton looked at him. "By God, I'll have to see that! I've made some purty good touch-offs in my day, but nary a one that'd shoot fifty yards, nor hit a turkey's head, neither!"

Rady's hands were sweating and he kept rubbing them down the sides of his pants. "Well, I don't aim to be braggin' nor nuthin'," he said, "but I *think* I kin hit it from here."

"Whaddya use, buckshot?"

"Yessir."

Ed handed him back his gun. "Go ahead an' shoot, kid. An' by God if you even touch that there bird, hit's yore'n!"

The men all shouted for him to go ahead, so he rammed a buckshot down the barrel and squared away. He never used a rest and there wasn't no sight on his barrel. He just stood up there and cocked her. He looked awful little in the midst of all those men. And his red hair was kinked all over his head like copper corkscrews. His eyes were hard and unblinking when he sighted down the barrel, but his face had paled so that his freckles stood out yellow and thick across his nose. He waited as still as a tree on a windless day till the turkey quit weaving its head, then he let her fly. The gobbler squawked and ducked, giving proof he'd hit it, and the men tore out to see, Ed Bruton in the lead. "He hit it! They ain't no doubts about it," he yelled, and there were others shouting the same thing. "He burned it," they said, "fair scorched it!"

Rady himself never went to see. I don't reckon he could of, hardly, his knees was trembling so. He just kind of leaned up against a tree and waited. Ed came back carrying the turkey. "I'd like you all to see some real shootin', men," he says, holding up the bird. "Take a look!"

They crowded around. Rady hadn't by no means killed the bird, of course. Neither had he come close to putting out its eye. But his buckshot had drilled a neat little hole right through two folds of the old gobbler's wattles! And with a touch-off, that's kind of good shooting!

"Here you are, son," Ed said, handing him the turkey. "I'm as good as my word. I said if you touched it, hit was yore'n, an' by God, hit's yore'n!"

"Is it mine to do with what I want?" Rady asked.

"Hit shore is! Hit'll be good eatin', too, come Thanksgiving!"

Rady shook his head. "No, sir. I ain't aimin' on takin' it home. I'd like to raffle it off here amongst the men, if you wouldn't keer."

"What you want to raffle it off fer?" Ed said.

"I want to git me a real gun."

But he never had to raffle it off. Old Grampa Jett offered to trade him his muzzle-loader for the turkey and Rady took him up on it. Grampa said he was getting too old to shoot anyways, couldn't even hit the side of a barn no more, and he might as well trade his gun for a good mess of turkey.

So that's how Rady came by his muzzle-loading rifle, and he couldn't of been no prouder of it if it had of been brand-new. He went prancing off home with it over his shoulder feeling like Dan'l Boone must of felt when he kilt the b'ar! Of course he got a licking for sneaking off to the turkey shoot. His old man took the harness straps to him that night, but Rady had his gun and that's what he'd gone for. He give it to me a while back and I've still got it. You can put a squirrel's eye out with it to this day if you're a mind to and a good enough shot.

He came by the hound dog some easier. It just come a stray to their house and took up. Just a common, ordinary black and tan hound, sway-backed, flop-eared, splay-footed, with a long rope of a tail that wagged all the time. Rady liked the looks of him right off, though. He took him out across the field and watched him jump a rabbit, and when the dog tongued and Rady heard his deep old mouth, and watched him lay down on the rabbit and stay with it, he knew he'd come across a real hound dog, a hunting dog.

"We got dogs enough already," his old man told him. "An' this here un's jist another wuthless hound. No good'll ever come of him. Can't be feedin' no more dogs."

"Ain't none of the dogs we got already has caught that big gray fox has been raidin' the henhouse, have they?"

Old man Cromwell peered at him. "No, nor that'n won't neither!"

"If he does, kin I keep him?"

"If he does, you kin keep him!"

So a couple of nights later me and Rady tried our hand at getting the big gray one. We commenced at the head of the holler and worked down. He had to cross that holler to get to the henhouse. Old Drum raced on ahead of us, sniffing and snuffing. We went plumb down one side the holler and back up the other without Drum one time hitting a trail. But he was sure working hard. We'd just decided the old gray one was staying home that night when off up the ridge ahead of us Drum gave tongue, a long, low bell-tone that settled right down into the steady yipping of the trail. We stopped where we were to follow the direction. The fox was keeping to the ridge-top, where it was thickety and rough, but we could tell from the way Drum was keeping steady he wasn't having no trouble. Rady let out a big sigh. "They's nothin' to do now but wait an' see," he said, and I knew what he meant. You can't help a dog stick to the trail. He's got to do it for himself. Either he can or he can't, and Rady was betting Old Drum would. If he lost the fox, then he'd just have to move on.

We stayed still and listened. They went on up the ridge until Drum's voice was just a whisper, and we were just thinking we'd better angle off up that way. Then he commenced to circle back. "Where you think he'll cross?" Rady said.

"The old field at the head of the holler?" I wondered.

Rady said so too, so we took off. But we soon changed our minds, for we could hear Drum, still steady, circling yon side the holler. We stopped. "He's makin' fer the branch," Rady said. A fox'll try to lose a hound by crossing and recrossing water, and many a good hound can be lost that way. We slid down the ridge into the holler and waited. Now was about the worst time of all. If Drum fooled around and lost the fox in the water, he'd have time to get away from the dog. But the dog was smart too. He wasted no time crossing the water. He knew the fox as well as the fox knew dogs, and he wasn't bothered none when the fox's scent went into the water. He never tried to cross. He just stuck his nose down and went right on up the branch till he hit the trail again where the fox had come back out. Instead of the fox gaining, he'd lost ground! And Drum was right on him when he came out on this side. "Come on!" Rady yelled at me then, "he'll make for the rock-slide now!"

I'd been thinking the same thing, for that would likely be his next trick, to try to lose the hound on rock. We lit out and got there while the fox was still circling. There wasn't much moon, but there was enough. Across that piece of bare rock we couldn't help seeing the fox. We huddled down behind a shoulder and waited. Directly we knew Drum had headed him and they were coming this way. Rady got his gun ready and stood, and when the fox hit the rock-slide and slowed a little, he pulled the trigger. The fox yelped, flung itself into the air and twisted, then fell of a heap. And Drum was right on him, shaking him and growling deep in his throat.

"All right, boy," Rady was pulling him off. "All right, now. Good boy. Good dog!" patting him and talking to him. He was mighty pleased with the dog, and he had reason to be. A man and his dog, hunting, are like partners working together. They've got to understand one another, and they've both got to be dependable. A man has got to know, from the way his dog works, what he's doing and what to expect. A dog has got to know a man knows what to do. It wouldn't do a dog no good to work his heart out if he was hunting with a damn fool.

Rady hoisted the fox and packed it home with him, and the old man kept his word. "You kin keep the hound," he said. "I've give my word on it."

So Rady and Drum found their partnership that night, and till the day Drum died they kept it.

And the way he got his gittar was by digging sang and selling it. Ginseng grows wild hereabouts and the roots, dried, have always brought a good price. The same companies that buy fur pelts buy sang, and I've heard it's shipped to China where there's a heap of store set by it for medicine. Anyways, all us hill boys had always made spending money by digging it all summer and fall, drying it out and selling it.

Rady'd always liked to sing and whistle a tune. Seemed like he had a natural ear for music. And he saw a gittar in the mail-order book one day that he took a shine to. I recollect it was priced at $10.95. His old man hit the roof. "What in tarnation you want with a gittar? Can't play it. An' that's a heap of money to be a-throwin' away on a useless instrument!"

"I kin learn to play it." Rady said, stubborn-like.

"Well, you'll not be buyin' no gittar with none of *my* money!" his pa told him.

"Don't aim to. I'll *make* the money."

But it takes a heap of sang to weigh out ten dollars worth. When it dries and the moisture evaporates, it gets mighty light. It took him the whole season, digging every spare minute he had, and traveling many a mile up and down the hollers to find enough. But he stayed with it, and he finally had it. He made out the order himself, chewing his pencil trying to figure out the postage rates. A set of lessons come with it, and he allowed they'd help him a heap in learning.

It was a Saturday when the gittar come, but the old man never said nothing about it till the day's end, figuring Rady'd scant his work if he knew. But when supper was over he brung it out and gave it over to him. Everybody gathered around to see it, and Rady was so excited he could hardly open the box. There it was, brown and shiny and new-looking. "Why, hit's not strung!" Rady said, disappointed at first.

"Shore not," the old man said. "The strings'd likely pop durin' its travels. You got to string it yerself."

The directions were there, though, plain as day, and in no time Rady had it strung. Then he opened out the first lesson, with the drawings to show where to put his fingers. He propped it up in front of him, and he commenced learning to play the gittar. It took him all that evening to learn the chords to that first lesson, for his hands were big and awkward. He learned them, though, and when he got through he was kind of trembling all over. "I kin make music," he said. And he run his hand down the side of the gittar like he was smoothing it. "I kin make music."

So Rady had the three things he wanted most. His gun . . . his dog . . . and his gittar. That tells a heap about him. But not all. The fourth thing he learned to love never came till later . . . but it lasted the longest.

Chapter Two

Rady's folks lived down on Old Ridge . . . the one that was first settled. The main part of the settlement drifted over this way in time and centered here on New Ridge. Not many folks live on Old Ridge any more, and didn't even when Rady was a boy. It's a sharp, narrow spur that angles off south from New Ridge and it was always a scant and meager place, heavy-timbered right up to the rim of the ridge and gullied by a dozen hollers. Reckon the reason it was settled first was on account of when you came up from the river bottoms it was handy. But there wasn't much room to lay out a field, and the fields weren't worth much when you got them laid out. So the settlement drifted this way because of the heavy timber, the hollers and the poorness of the land. There's always been two or three families, though, that liked it over on Old Ridge or couldn't do any better. Rady's pa was one of them.

He had around sixty acres of as poor land as the hills ever turn loose of. Wasn't a field but what a man grew spraddle-legged trying to plow, and the house set on the side of a hill so steep you wondered what kept it from sliding off. You went down four steps to go into the front door, and the back room was so high off the ground that the old man drove his wagon under it for a shed. It was a rackety kind of house at that. Two rooms deep, with a lean-to on the back, and a kind of loft-room overhead. The boys slept in the loft-room. There was a ladder built in one corner of the fireplace room that went up to it. The old man, a miserly kind of old fellow, used to chase the boys up to bed when good dark come. Never would set up past dark on account of having to burn a lamp. "No use wastin' oil," he'd say. "Man ort to git his business tended to of a day. No need borrowin' from the night." The only time the lamps were ever lit was of a morning. The old man stirred soon, and roused the kids out by three-thirty in the summertime, and four o'clock in the winter. "Never could abide a body liked to lay," he said. "My opinion, he's a wuthless kind of a man."

Rady's pa looked like he'd stepped right out of the Old Testament. He stood six-foot-tall barefooted, and I reckon he'd of weighed two hundred, stripped. Regular giant of a man. He had little, sharp, black eyes and a rabbity kind of nose. Twitched on the end, times. His hair was stiff, like it had been starched and stood up coarse and ropey on his head. Wasn't white. Was gray. And what gave him the look of a prophet more than anything else was his beard. He was the only man I ever knew still wore a long beard. It was gray, too.

And there were other ways in which he was like one of the old patriarchs. He believed in the multiplication of his seed, I reckon, for he raised up a sight of kids, not to call him blessed exactly, for they never did. But to work his gravelly, rocky fields for him as long as he could hold them to it. He worked his young'uns awful hard. And the most they ever got out of it was a place to sleep, something to eat and a few cheap clothes. Old Man Cromwell come as nigh making his kids into work animals as anybody I ever saw.

Besides farming, he felt called to preach the Word of a Sunday, and he held with the primitive, foot-washing, shouting-and-singing kind of religion common to the hills. He was a sight to see in the pulpit. Used to wonder how he had a hair left in that beard of his, the way he used to pull at it when he got up steam in his preaching. But there was a kind of slow dignity about the old man when he got up to step into the pulpit. His hair was slicked down and parted. His shirt was white and clean. He always wore his best black coat. His Sunday coat. And he commenced slow-like, weighing his words and bearing down on the congregation with his sharp, old, beady eyes like he was seeking sin in everybody there. Like it was hiding in the corners and if he looked sharp enough he'd find it. Then he'd commence to sweat a little and the words would come a mite faster. About the time he ripped his coat off, he was really getting under the power. Then he'd pound the pulpit, the words pouring out his mouth and the froth and the foam of his spit mixing with them. The sweat would slick his face and run down his neck, wilting his white collar. Soon or late he'd tear that collar off, but it wasn't till the buttons went to popping loose on his shirt front that he was what you might say at his top speed. From then on his eyes kind of glazed over and his head jerked and he yanked at his beard and poured it on. A good hill preacher, at his best, goes a lot like a tobacco auctioneer. Folks that's used to it can follow him, but if you've not heard a hill preacher when he's gospel-happy, it wouldn't make much sense to you. It goes too fast, and there's too many "ahs" in it. "I tell you-ah- my brethern-ah- hit don't make no diffrunce-ah- when the Lord-ah- comes to judge his own-ah- the sheep-ah- will be separated-ah- from the goats-ah- and the Lord-ah- will judge-ah- them that's his own-ah- and you better-ah- make mighty shore-ah- that you'll-ah- not be amongst-ah- the goats-ah!"

That was a favorite theme of Old Man Cromwell's . . . the sheep and the goats. And it always made Rady mad. "Old goat hisself," he'd mutter under his breath. "He'll have to go home an' lay Marty to git it all outen his system!"

Marty was Rady's stepmother. She was the old man's third wife. Rady was the second oldest boy. His ma had died before he could remember, and before he could remember, either, the old man had married Sturmy Jones. He'd wore her out in less than ten years, and before she was cold in the ground, he'd married her sister Marty. Marty was on her fourth kid now. She was, as Rady put it, pregnant as hell all the time.

A lot of the hill preachers have big families. I've often wondered about it. But I reckon Rady put his finger on it. There must be something about religious fervor that kindles something else. Kindles it, but stops short, so that when a guy works up a lather about religion he's got to top it off by going to bed before he's wholly satisfied. It works that way for a lot that's in the congregation too. During revivals in the summertime there been many a couple got all hot and bothered under the spell of the preacher and took to the bushes to cool off. More than one young'un hereabouts owes his life to a revival meeting!

It was tedious setting through the old man's long-winded sermons of a Sunday morning. He held forth a couple of hours most times, and has been known to go three. We used to sit on the back row and get so bench-worn we could hardly heave ourselves up when meeting broke up. One morning Rady pulled out his penny for the collection plate and commenced tossing it and slapping it down on the back of his hand. I was setting next and I got mine out and slapped it down. "Heads," I called it, and Rady nodded. It was tails, so he took it. The boy next to me saw what was going on so he hauled his penny out. He won and Rady passed him the penny. They matched again, and he lost. Again, and he was without pennies. Rady eased down on the floor so as to reach across to the next guy, and took his penny too. That's all we ever had for collection. Pennies. One each, that is. There was about eight of us on the back row, and before the plate come around Rady had all our pennies. I never thought but what he'd put them in the plate, but when Lem passed it, Rady dropped in his own penny, solemn as an owl, and that was all. The rest of us could of gone through the floor when we had to pass the plate along emptyhanded. Lem's eyebrows shot up and his face got long, but of course all he suspicioned was we were holding out to buy candy with.

We jumped Rady when we got outside. "Hey, we wasn't matchin' for keeps!"

"I was," he said, "an' when you match with me, you better be!"

The next Sunday morning we wouldn't match, on account of we knew Lem Milford would say something to our folks if we missed putting in two times hand-going. When the plate came down the row I saw Rady drop his in, but I also saw his little finger flip two or three coins up into the palm of his hand. I tried it, too, and got by with it. After Lem had taken the plate up front, me and Rady passed the pennies around and showed the rest how we'd got them. Now that we had a way to get enough money to match with, the time passed a heap quicker.

But we had to quit matching pennies with the collection money after John Orson got caught. Lem caught the kid red-handed. Made him open out his palm and spill the pennies right in front of everybody. The kid went to sniveling. "They all do it," he said, smearing snot over his face with his shirt-sleeve. "They do it all the time. But this is the first time I ever done it." Which was a lie. He'd been doing it as long as we had, but was just clumsy.

Old man Cromwell come charging down the center aisle like a bull after a red flag. "Rady Cromwell!" he thundered, "stand up there!"

Rady stood up. He was just about as cool as a cucumber.

"You know anything about this?"

"Yessir," Rady said, never batting an eye, "the kid's been snitchin' pennies outen the collection plate right along. Not only pennies but nickels an' dimes when he could git 'em. Fur as I know, none of the rest is in it."

"He's a-lyin', he's a-lyin'!" the Orson kid yelled.

"What have the rest of you boys got to say?" the old man said, turning to us and letting his eyes run over us hard and bright.

"Rady's right, sir," I said, and the others joined in.

"It's like Rady said, sir."

"Yessir. Rady's got the straight of it."

We lied. And thought nothing of it. We'd of stood by the kid if he hadn't of squirmed on us. But Rady was right. "Hell," he said, "a guy won't stand by the rest ortent to be stood by. Let him take what's comin' to him!"

So the Orson kid got the skin beat off his back twice. Once by his old man, and the next day by Rady. But it was Rady knocked his tooth out. He never did have that tooth put back in, and every time I ever saw John Orson from then on and got a glimpse of that vacant space in his teeth, it reminded me of the beating Rady had give him. He like to of killed him. But that ended our penny-snatching.

Rady had a busy mind, though. He was like a rat gnawing in a corn crib. When he got through with one ear, he commenced on another one. He figured a deal on the schoolbooks next. "Wanna make a dime?" he asked the little kids.

"Shore!"

"O.K. Drop yer reader by the big beech tree this evening."

"What fer?"

"You wanna make a dime or don't you?"

Most of them did, so they dropped their books by the beech tree. Then Rady took them to the bookstore in town and sold them. Sold them cheap, I reckon, for two-bits maybe or thirty cents. But that was good profit, for he was only out a dime on each book.

"Where you gettin' these books?" the bookstore man asked him one day when he took three or four in to sell. I reckon he thought Rady was stealing them.

"I buy 'em," Rady told him, and that wasn't no lie.

"Well, you can quit buyin' 'em," the man said, "this is the last lot I'm goin' to take off your hands. There's been several in here the past week or two complaining of their kids losing their books might regular."

"They're gittin' paid," Rady said.

The man looked at him sharp over his glasses. "Listen, sonny. The kids may be gittin' paid, but their folks is payin' twice. Don't bring no more in here, see!"

But Rady made a dollar and a half before that deal folded.

He got into trouble once though. He talked his kid sister into letting the guys see her with her pants down for a nickel a peek. Promised her half they took in. Then he tried to hold out for two-thirds. Said he was the one went out and worked up the trade! But she was a big operator too, so she raised so much hell and made so much noise Marty caught on. Then Marty told the old man and he horse-whipped Rady. When he got through whipping him he rubbed salt in the welts and Rady's back was sore for a month. But what he minded most was that after the whipping the old man took him in the house and set him down and read the Bible to him. All the places that talk about fornication and nakedness and whores and harlots. Rady said that was the part of the Bible the old man liked best anyways. Being religious like he was he couldn't let his mind dwell on such things most times. It wouldn't of been right. But what was in the Bible was holy. And a man could fill his soul on fornication with the blessing of the Lord just by knowing the right places to read.

"I never minded the beatin'," Rady said. "I had that comin' to me, I reckon. But hit made me sick to my stummick to have to set there an' listen to the old sunovabitch read the Bible. Makin' it sound so holy an' all the time rollin' the words around in his mouth like they was a chew of tobaccer! Christ, but the Bible is a filthy book!"

I reckon that's one reason why Rady wasn't never what you'd call a religious man. Got turned against it early.

He learned to shoot craps from the niggers down in the river bottoms. The rest of us learned from him. Same with stud poker. We used to sneak off down in the holler back of the church and play poker with a deck of greasy old cards he got hold of, and shoot craps on a saddle blanket off Jubal Moore's old mule. Didn't any of us have but a few nickels to rattle around in our overhalls pockets, but the way they changed from our pockets to Rady's was a sight to see!

Down in the holler, too, was where most of us took our first drink of moonshine. Rady showed up with a gallon jug one night. We must of all been around sixteen then. "Ten cents a drink," he said, and started the jug passing.

"Whaddya mean ten cents a drink?" we argued.

"Lissen," he said, "any of you goops got a buck an' a half to pay fer a jug?"

We hadn't.

"So it's ten cents a drink, see!"

But he never pulled that on us but once. We chipped in and bought the next jug ourselves. And I reckon it coming so cheap was what made most of us get pretty drunk the next Saturday night. Was a revival meeting going on, it being summertime, and there was a mess of people there. The meeting was being held in a tent pitched out in the churchyard, with the sides rolled up on account of the heat. We never went in, of course. Wasn't but a few fellers our age got religion sufficiently to set through them sermons. But we always went. We'd go down in the holler and shoot craps by lantern light until the shouting commenced, and then knowing the meeting was breaking up soon we'd light out back up the hill. Most of us had a girl we wanted to walk home.

That Saturday night, though, we tasted the jug right regular and being unused to drinking much we got in a fair way of being likkered. Enos Higgins made a fiery brand of moonshine and it never took much to unsettle a man's head. For my part I couldn't see the spots on the dice long before Rady had the idea to break up the meeting.

"Whose shotgun is that?" Rady asked, nodding towards a gun leaning up against a tree off to one side.

"Mine," Duke Simmons said.

"What you bring a gun to meetin' fer?"

"Come early through the woods. Figgered I might git a shot at a squirrel."

Rady rammed a hand in his pocket and brought out a fist full of bird shot. He sifted it from one hand to another, letting the shot trickle through soft and rattly, like rain on a shingle roof. "Jubal Moore's old mule hitched at the same place tonight?" he asked.

Everybody commenced grinning. Duke pulled out a shell and Rady fixed it. "Head him towards the tent," he said. "Ever'body mix an' mingle with the stampede. Don't nobody run away."

Duke turned the mule with a handful of corn shucks and then got away quick. The shot never sounded very loud, of course, but man, when it hit that mule he let out a bray you could of heard to King's Crossing and back! And then he commenced running!

When he trumpeted off everybody in the tent jumped a foot high and then when they turned and saw that mule headed for the tent there was the almightiest lot of screeching and bellowing ever you heard! Folks tried to climb the tent poles. They clawed up on top one another! And they got down on all fours and scrooched in under the benches. The preacher took one look and then he tried to crawl in the pulpit. He got in, too, all but his backside, and that being a mite on the bulgy side, it just stuck there and wiggled while he prayed! The choir, robes and all, took to the timber, and it was like a flapping of mighty wings! Man, man!

That old mule lit out across them benches, braying and bucking and pawing the ground. He split a couple of them into right sizable pieces of cook wood. He sure cut a real wide swath through that tent, and kept right on going over the ridge. Jubal never found him till the next day, and then he was easing his sore behind in old man Crimmer's cow pond! Such a commotion!

We come up fast on the tail of the mule and mixed with the crowd, acting just as scared and just as bewildered as the worst of them. Wasn't a one of us missing, and when the folks quietened down some it was Rady lifted a righteous voice. "Who could of done sich a thing? Who would think of breakin' up a meetin' thisaway! Hit must of been the Bruton boys!"

There was a heap of talk, naturally. And a few looks cast our way. But there we were, as innocent as could be, right in their midst. So, in general, it was decided the Bruton boys had done it. They had the name of going around breaking up meetings like that. We saw the oldest one over at the county seat a couple of weeks after that.

"Wouldn't visit around over on New Ridge fer a time," Rady told him.

The guy grinned. "Sunovabitch," he said, "we never broke up that meetin'."

"I never said you did," Rady told him, "but they's several that thinks so."

"We don't use mules," the Bruton fellow said.

Rady walked off, but over his shoulder he called back, "Try one sometime. Hit's a heap more excitin' than pistol shots!"

He was always promoting something, Rady was. I got to thinking about it one time and it looked to me like most of us lined his pockets considerably one way or another when we were kids. A dime here, two-bits there. He did business with anybody and everybody. And he did almost any kind of business. A penny in his pocket wasn't small potatoes to him. It was a penny, and it was his. By the time he was fourteen he was running a regular junk yard. He'd buy anything anybody had for sale, if he could rake and scrape up enough to buy it with. And most times he could. An old bicycle rim. . . a broken down cook stove . . . a wheelbarrow without the wheel. One way or another he always had something to trade with, and he always come out on top in a trade. He knew how to take things to pieces and sell every last bolt and screw for scrap.

Once folks thought sure he'd been suckered. He went around buying up old tables and chairs. Give as high as three dollars apiece for them. But they'd ought to figured he knew what he was doing. Was an antique buyer in the county seat and he bought everything Rady brought him, and gave him good money for it. When folks found out about it they kind of complained. "You'd ort to of told us, Rady," they said. "You hadn't ort to of done so to us. Hit wasn't hardly right."

"Why wasn't it?" he said. "you thought three dollars was a good price when I give it to you. Snickered behindst my back . . . figgered you'd got the best of me. A guy ain't smart enough to figger a trade ain't got no business tradin' is what I say."

"That Rady Cromwell," folks would say, and they couldn't help laughing over some of his deals, "that Rady Cromwell is a cute one. Plumb shrewd he is. He'll allus come out on top."

He was a likable guy, even when he sharped you. And there wasn't nobody but what had to admit he sharped them clean. He never cheated. He hated a cheat. He was just smarter than most in a trade, and there wasn't nothing wrong with outsmarting a man. Fact is, if you let a man get the best of you in a trade, it was a thing to be ashamed of. Rady had little to his shame, though.

When he got his full growth, around seventeen, he wasn't as tall as his old man, but he was built powerful through the shoulders and neck like him. And his legs were as solid as piano posts. He was kind of short-legged and he had a way of standing spraddled, like he'd grown right out of the ground. He was weighted well, too. Never no paunch on him, but he was fleshed out considerable. He wasn't to say handsome, but he wasn't bad-looking, either. His hair was a brownish-red, thick, and I reckon you'd call it curly. Kind of bushed up like the old man's. His eyes were blue, a kind of flinty, bright blue, and he could hold a man's look unblinking longer than anybody I ever saw. It was never Rady's eyes dropped first.

He had a heavy beard, but he never let it go after he commenced to shave, like the rest of us did. Most of us don't shave but once a week here on the ridge. But Rady said he couldn't abide the feel of his beard growing, so he shaved every day. Had a smooth, thick skin, not like the thin white kind that commonly goes with red hair. When he was little he freckled, but when he grew up the freckles faded. When he got mad, though, seemed like the blood drained out of his face and you could see half a dozen freckles standing out on his nose. We used to know when we were joking him too far by the way his freckles'd commence showing. And we had a kind of joke about it. We'd say, "Look out! Rady's freckles is showin'!"

What I always liked about Rady was his good-natured ways. He could take a joke as easy as he could give one, and he had a hearty and a ready laugh. He had a hell of a temper when he was crossed, but he never let go of it much. He like to of killed that Orson kid for telling on us that time, and I've seen him beat a mule down to its knees for being stubborn. But most times he went along pretty even-tempered. He'd stop and pass the time of day with anybody, tell his share of tall tales, talk you out of your ready cash, laugh over a dirty joke, and pass on, nobody the worse for it. The menfolks made room for him on the long bench down at the store, and the womenfolks . . . well, some of them made room for him too when he wanted. In more private places.

Rady was no stallion, but then neither was he any gelding. He learned early like the rest of us, took what come his way, bragged a little over his doings, and kept it where it belonged. Something to enjoy when there was opportunity and maybe to make the opportunity if encouraged. But not a thing to get all hot and bothered about. A healthy man knows what to do about his wants. Satisfy them if he can, and if he can't, he knows he can sweat them out behind a plow. A full day's plowing will take care of most anything!

Rady was a little different from the rest of us though. Most of us talked to one girl, got stuck on her and thought we was in love. Over and over it happened. Myself, I had ten girls in ten months one year. But Rady never singled out one girl to talk to. And he never appeared to care which one he was with. Made no fuss over none of them. And if she went in the bushes with him, he never seemed to have no personal feeling about it. Quick to heat, quick to satisfy, quick to forget. I've seen him walk away from a girl when he was through and never give her a backward look. I asked him once if he didn't ever care anything about the girl herself.

"Why?" he said.

"Well, I allus feel different about some girls," I said.

"I don't," he said. "What's one got that the other'n ain't?"

But he got mad as a hornet just the same the first time he was with Susie Bratton. "Goddammit!" he said, telling us, "you know what she done? Right in the middle she reached up an' picked a ripe blackberry an' eat it!"

"She don't eat no blackberries with me!" Duke Simmons bragged.

"You think you're better'n I am, is that it?"

Duke kind of snickered. "Must be. But Susie Bratton shore as hell don't pick no blackberries when *I'm* with her!"

Rady hit him before the words had hardly got out of his mouth. Hit him square in the mouth and mashed his teeth into his lips. He fell and rolled over a time or two, but he got up fighting. The trouble with Duke was he liked a knife too good, and when he got up his knife was out. Before Rady could grapple him he'd slashed quick and the knife sliced Rady's neck. Not deep, but it took the hide. He's got the scar from it to this day. But Duke got only that one slash in, for Rady got his wrist in them big hands of his and broke it clean in two. It cracked like a chestnut log in a hot fire! Duke crumpled and groaned. "You've broke it," he said.

"I aimed to. Don't never draw no knife on me agin, Duke. You kin save that fer the Bruton boys."

Then he went with Duke to the doctor to have the wrist set.

The doctor eyed them while he was working on Duke. "You boys been fighting?"

"No sir," Duke said. "We was wrastlin' an' we kind of fell over a rough place. Rady here, skint his neck, an' I landed on my wrist."

The doctor kind of humphed, knowing better I reckon, but he set Duke's wrist and painted Rady's neck with some kind of medicine.

We figured Duke and Rady needed some kind of relief from the pain of a knife slash and a broken wrist, so we picked up a jug of moonshine on the way home. Rady was riding double with me and he was nursing the jug. Must of sampled it right frequent too, for when we got to the holler he was bellering for his gittar. "I want my gittar!" he kept yelling. "Duke, go git my gittar!"

"I got a broke wrist," Duke said, "I ain't goin' to climb that ridge. Go git it yerself!"

I was building a little fire to keep the night chill off. "You go git it," Rady says, turning to me.

"What's the matter with you goin'?" I says.

"All right, I'll go git it," he says, and he stumbled off a few steps. "But if I don't come back," he says, kind of tragic, "hit'll be on account the old man has smelt this here likker on me an' has done kilt me!"

So I went and got it for him. Had to slip in, but the folks had done laid down, so all I had to do was sneak in the fireplace room and pick it up. While I was gone Rady and Duke'd raided a cornfield and had a dozen ears roasting in the ashes. They smelled powerful good. I handed Rady his gittar. "Now you got to sing for yer supper," I told him.

"That suits me," he says, and he rared back and commenced.

He sung "Barby Allen" and "On Top of Old Smokey." And he sung "The Blackest Crow" and "Turtle Dove." The tunes were sad and sweet and Rady's gittar was soft underneath the words, smoothing and holding them up. I've always liked those old song-ballats. I'd heard my grandma sing them time and time again. And I said so, when Rady stopped singing.

Rady nodded his head. "All them song-ballats goes way back.

I ordered me some song books awhile back, but don't none of 'em have ary song-ballats in 'em. Reckon folks must of jist allus sung 'em. But I like 'em a heap."

"They're too sad an' mournful fer me," Duke says, throwing a chunk of wood on the fire. "They's allus somebody a-dyin'! You take that there one you sing about Lord Thomas an' Fair Elinore! That un's plumb tearful! One girl a-killin' another'n, an' Lord Thomas a-killin' the one that's left, an' then a-killin' hisself! Jist a mess of killin's! That un jist don't make sense!"

Rady swung the jug up and took a big swaller. Then he picked up his gittar again. "I like it though," he says.

> Lord Thomas rose early one day in May
> An' dressed hisself in blue;
> Says, "Mother I'm goin' to git married today,
> An' I want advice from you."

"Now, that's what I mean," Duke says. "Ary man's a man ain't goin' to git advice from his ma to git married! He'd jist go git married!"

> The brown girl, she has house an' land,
> Fair Elinore, she has none.
> "Therefore, I charge you with my blessin's
> Go bring the brown girl home."

"An' the old bag tellin' him to git the brown girl, shore. On account of her havin' a house an' land!"

Rady's shoulders shook as he laughed. "Twan't sich bad advice, Duke. Mebbe the old girl knowed what was best fer her boy."

> He rode 'til he come to fair Elinore's gate,
> An' he rattled at the ring;
> There was no one more ready than she
> To rise up an' let him in.

Rady kept picking as he talked. "I've allus wondered what that meant. 'Rattlin' at the ring.'"

"Reckon he could of had a ring in his pocket he rattled," Duke said. "Don't make no sense anyways!"

"Oh, what's the matter, Lord Thomas," she cried,
"Oh, what's the matter with you?"
"I've come to invite you to my weddin',
Ain't that good news to you?"

"Oh, mother, shall I go to Lord Thomas' weddin',
Or shall I tarry at home?"
"Therefore, I charge you with my blessin's,
You'd better tarry at home."

"An' she shore had better of," Duke said. "Jist look what happened to her!"

She dressed herself in her best,
An' most of her dressin' was green.
An' ever' village that she rode through
They took her to be some queen.

She rode 'til she come to Lord Thomas' gate,
An' rattled at the ring;
There was none more ready than he
To rise up and let her in.

"What I can't understand," said Rady, feathering the gittar, "is why, if they loved one another so good he ever takened her home. Both of 'em ready to rise up an' let one another in! Both of 'em rattlin' at the ring! Looks like he'd of jist swung fair Elinore up behindst him on his mule an' rode off with her."

"He hadn't no backbone was why," Duke says. "He was skeered of his ma."

"I reckon hit was the house an' land looked too good to him," Rady says.

He took her by the lily-white hand
An' led her in the hall;
An' seated her there at the head of the table
Amongst the gentlemen all.

"Is this yore bride, sits here at yer side?
I'm shore she's wonderful brown!
You might have married as fine a young lady
As ever the sun shone on."

"Now this here's the crazy part," Duke muttered. "This is the part I wouldn't give ten cents fer."

The brown girl, she had a knife,
It was both long and sharp.
She pierced it into fair Elinore's side,
An' it entered into her heart.

"Oh, what's the matter, fair Elinore?" he cried,
"Oh, what's the matter with you?"
"Oh, don't you see my own heart's blood
A-trinklin' down my side?"

"'Oh, what's the matter, fair Elinore?'" Duke mocked, "An' pierced through the heart like she was, she had the breath to say her blood was trinklin' down her side!"
"Shut up!" I said, "an' let Rady git it over with."

He took the brown girl by the hand
An' led her by the wall;
An' there with a sword, he cut off her head
An' dashed it agin the wall.

Sayin', "Here's the death of three true loves,
God send their souls to rest;
Bury the brown girl at my feet,
An' fair Elinore at my breast."

"See!" Duke says, "see how crazy hit goes!"
"Hit's jist a song," Rady said. "But hit tells a right good story, an' the music's slow an' sweet. I like it."
"Well, I don't!"

"The corn's ready," I told them. And between the roasting ears and the jug of moonshine we had no more time for song-ballats that night.

Oh, we were wild all right. There's no doubts about it. Wild and pranky and a heap of trouble sometimes. But we were wild the way young animals are wild. Wild by instinct and by necessity. Just full of our own bigness, busting out the seams with it, healthy and feeling fine and having to boil over, times. There wasn't nothing mean in our wildness. Not never. We were hearty and whole, loving to eat and drink and make love. We worked hard, we drank hard, and I reckon we fornicated hard. Me, I could never see anything wrong with it. Adds up pretty good in my catalogue. Take a young feller, green and full of his own juices, and make him healthy and untwisted and unsoured, and you got about as fine a being as the Lord ever created . . . perfect, that is, for his own uses and his own purposes, in his own time and place. We were like that. And it was all fun and fine. Looking back on it now, and remembering, I'd say, even, it was the best.

Chapter Three

He was seventeen the year he tended Annie Abbott's tobacco for her. Seventeen, and quite a buckaroo. He was like a hickory sapling, tough and apt to bend in the wind without breaking. Sweet, the way anything young and tender is sweet, and stout and whole and sound.

Annie was Harm Abbott's woman, but he'd been dead going on a year then. I reckon she must of been around thirty-five, although I don't know as anybody would think of how old she was one way or the other. Far back as I could remember she'd been Harm Abbott's woman, and she was just Harm Abbott's widow now that he was gone. She was a right comely woman, as women of that age go. Not burden-bent nor ill, like is common to most ridge women. They never raised any young'uns, so when Harm died she was left by herself.

A woman left alone like that has got to do one of two things. She's either got to get married again, so's to have a man to work her place, or else she's got to get somebody to rent and tend it for her. Lige Sherman was already courting Annie, but she was taking her time about making up her mind. And properly so, for she had a right smart farm to bring a man, and it would pay her to think more than once.

She lived across the holler from Old Man Cromwell. Her

land laid a mite more level than most, and Harm had been a smart farmer. Kept his fields up good and never overworked them. He'd always raised good tobacco and corn, and had more in pastures than is common. Spent money on good seed and good fertilizer. The place showed it.

Rady was piling brush and burning his pa's tobacco bed when the idea come to him to tend Annie's patch for her. It had been a hard winter, lot of snow and ice, but it was fairing up considerably for March, and the ground was thawed down a right smart. Rady'd been at it since good day and he had a good, slow fire going on the bed and had stopped to make him a cigarette. He eased his flanks up against an old stump and was just setting there, letting his back muscles go slack and feeling the sun on his neck. He looked off across the holler and saw Annie come out the kitchen door, and then he heard her calling her little chickens. "Diddle-diddle-diddle-diddle," her voice come high and clear across the holler. She had on a pink dress and he could see her arm moving as she threw the chicken feed out. "Diddle-diddle-diddle-diddle," and there was a flock of white around her feet.

Rady was thinking she must of got her hens off early. For Marty hadn't taken off a single setting yet. But then Marty was slack in more ways than one. She was nearly always late with her chickens and late with her garden, too. Whereas Annie had the name of being awful smart that way.

Rady got to thinking who was going to tend Annie's tobacco that year. Lige, likely, he thought. It stood to reason he'd have the inside on it, him courting her and all. Rady was thinking it would sure be a good deal, all right. Lige'd make out good on it. "I'd like to tend it myself," he thought. "Even on the halves, it'd bring in considerable cash money."

He got up and raked some limbs towards the center of the fire, and spread them around some, and then it come to him maybe she hadn't give Lige the promise of it yet. If she hadn't cold out give Lige her word yet, maybe he could talk her into letting him tend it! And as quick as the idea come to him, he acted on it. He dropped his rake and pulled out and went loping across the holler to see her while the notion was still strong.

She was still out in the back yard when he got there, kind of out of breath from hauling up the hill. "Miz Abbott," he said, coming up behind her, "Miz Abbott, you got anybody promised to tend yer tobaccer this year yit?"

She jumped like she was shot and spilled the chicken feed all over out of her apron. "Land sakes, Rady! You give me the worst start! Comin' up on a body sudden like that an' from behindst! Now see what you've made me do! Spill all my ground corn!"

Rady looked down but the chickens were already hard at it so there was nothing to be done but leave them have it. "I'm sorry," he said, "I'll grind you some more."

She dusted her hands off. "No mind. Hit don't matter. They was jist about through, anyways. Jist leave it go."

"I never aimed to skeer you," Rady said. "But I had it on my mind so strong to ast you about yer tobaccer. You got somebody to tend it yit?"

"Well, I have an' I haven't . . . you might say." And then she sniffed the air a couple of times. "Now my dinner's burnin'! Come on in the house if you want to talk to me!"

Rady followed her inside and set down just within the door. It was her potatoes that had stuck and were burning. She put them in another pan and poured water over them and set them back on the stove. Then she started to get a stick of wood to build up the fire. The wood box was empty. "Ever'thing I turn my hand to this mornin' has went wrong," she fumed. "Some days jist don't seem like nothin' goes right!"

"I'll git you some wood," Rady said, and he ducked outside to bring in an armful.

She chucked up the fire and then she set down in a little, low-backed rocker over by the window and commenced fanning herself with her apron.

"Have you, Miz Abbott?" Rady asked again.

"Have I what? Oh . . . you was talkin' about the tobaccer. Lige has studied some on tendin' it, but I've not rightly made up my mind yit. He's got a big crop hisself, an' I dislike to resk it 'thout I know hit's goin' to be tended good. Harm allus done good with that patch an' I'd hate to see it fail. Mind, I don't say Lige wouldn't tend it good. I've no doubts he'd do the best he could, but like I say, he's got a awful big crop hisself, an' when I study on it, don't seem like he could do justice to mine an' his'n too, an' hit stands to reason he'd take keer of his'n first. Hit's been a fret to me, to know what to do."

"Let me tend it, Miz Abbott. I'll tend it good an' make you a fine crop. Jist as good as Harm ever made, I swear it!"

"You!" she said, her mouth flying open. "Why, yore pa keeps you kids so everlastin' hard at work you couldn't tend nothin' when he gits through with you. Lige'd have more time than you would!"

"Yes, ma'am, I could!" Rady said, and he was so anxious by that time his hands were shaking. "I could tend it all right. After I git through at Pa's ever'day. I'm awful stout, an' I don't git tard very easy. I'd make you a good crop, shore!"

Annie looked at him. He'd eased off his chair and was standing in the middle of the floor, his hands sweating and him rubbing the sweat off against his pants legs. He had on overhalls, slicked with dirt and sooted with fire. They were a mite too little for him, and they stretched tight across his chest and down across his short, stocky legs. Like always he stood a little spraddled, and the scissors of his legs went up and joined in the tight-spread crotch. His denim shirt was open at the neck, and the short, coarse hairs on his chest grew up into the opening and made a cushion that a woman's hand would maybe want to feel. Not just there but running on down, to see how far the cushion went. Exploring, feeling, and maybe tangling and pulling, finally. He had a smell of hickory smoke on him, and a smell of sweat, and a smell of man. He ran his hands through his hair and it kinked up in little corkscrews, rusty like old wire. Annie looked at him. "I dunno, Rady," she said, slow-like. "I dunno. You're built stout like you say, but a body kin do jist so much an' no more. Hit'd be takin' a awful chancet. More, hit looks to me, than I'd be takin' with Lige."

"No, ma'am. You see, Miz Abbott, Lige is gittin' old. He ain't, to say, stout no more. He's slowin' down a heap nowadays. Hadn't you taken notice? Why, he was puny most all the winter! Had that pleurisy pain in his chest, an' was down in his back several times. I've not never been sick a day in my life, Miz Abbott. I'm stout, an' I'm used to hard work. You know that! I could hold out to do it!"

She was setting there on the other side of the room in her little rocking chair, making pleats in her apron, thinking. She didn't say nothing for a time, and Rady watched her, setting there with her head bent down. All at once it come over him that she wasn't a old woman at all! He'd always thought of her as old as Methuselah. She might of been seventy for all of him. But when he was looking at her setting there, rocking back and forth just a little bit in her rocking chair, the wind from her rocking making some curls on her forehead blow away from her face, and her hands busy with her apron, he felt a kind of surprise to notice that her hair was shiny and black and soft-looking. And her face was smooth . . . smooth like new cream and just about the same color except for two red spots high up on her cheekbones. Why, she's a good-looking woman, he thought to himself. And not old at all! There was a kind of wilting down in his legs and his breath commenced quickening.

"I dunno, Rady," she said, then, and her tongue licked out at her upper lip, and her tongue was red and pointed, and it left her lip wet. Rady's hands were sweating now, but not about the tobacco crop.

She looked up at him, and his face went hot and he could tell it was getting red. For she'd caught him eyeing the neck of her dress which was turned in at the collar and went down low between her bosoms. They were big and full and where the dress laid between them was like a soft, white valley. Rady wanted to run his hand down that valley, and he was thinking how it would feel, when she looked up. Her face turned red, too, and she put up her hand and buttoned the dress up higher.

"Don't," Rady said, and he started towards her.

But she got up quick-like and went over to the water shelf and dipped out a drink of water. She stood there with the dipper in her hands like she was afraid to turn around. Rady went up behind her and slid his arms around her and cupped his hands under those full breasts. They were just as soft as he'd thought they'd be. She took a quick breath when she felt his arms, and kind of choked and let the dipper slide back in the water. He could feel her heart beating hard and strong under his hand. He commenced turning her around, and as he turned her he commenced working on the buttons of the dress. She sort of leaned up against him, curvey and soft so that he could feel her flesh giving under his own hardness, and then she sighed.

The way a ridge man approaches a woman, commonly, is just that neat and direct. He don't waste no words asking. He don't fool around being nice. He don't act like he wants one thing when they both know he wants another. He just gets down to work. Either a woman will or she won't. And there's just one way to find out.

Well . . . Annie would. With Rady, leastways. When he left that morning he had her promise he could tend her tobacco, and whilst there was nothing said about it . . . that wouldn't of been good manners . . . he knew he could have Annie too when he wanted. "Hell," he told us, laughing about it, "she wanted a man. Harm's been dead a year or more. An' I wanted her tobaccer crop. You can't beat a trade like that." And then he kind of let his breath out long. "God , no, you shore can't beat a trade like that! Take a woman growed . . . knows what she's doin'! She's . . . she's . . ."

"You sure you kin hold out, Rady?" one of the boys asked, snickering. "That's goin' to be a heap of night work!"

Rady laughed. "That's what I like about it! An' don't go gittin' no idees I need any help!"

Well, I said he was a horse-trader. And he always came out on top. The rest of us were pretty disgusted with ourselves for not thinking of it first. And knowing how he was set up that season we watched him with considerable envy. But I have to admit there probably wasn't a one of us could of made the grade. Rady wasn't the old man's boy for nothing!

The summer slowed along, hot and muggy, the best season we'd had for tobacco in several years. Everybody's tobacco did well, but Rady's did better than anybody's. That patch of Annie's was the prettiest tobacco ever I saw in my life! Rady stole his plants from the old man's bed, and he made sure to get the best ones. He got his manure from the old man's barn, and the best rotted, the most aged, went to the widow's. She'd sold her stock when Harm died, all but a milk cow and a few pigs and chickens, so she didn't have nothing for Rady to plow with. He tried to get the loan of the old man's team, but old man Cromwell wouldn't lend the team. So Rady hired a team to break the land. But after that he tended the crop by hand. Late of the evening after he got through at his pa's. For the old man let him know right off he wasn't going to have him slacking off his work at home. And I reckon he saw to it Rady came up to scratch. But we never felt sorry for him hoeing out that tobacco clean till moonup. We knew what was waiting for him inside when he laid his hoe down.

Many a time Annie got out there and helped him too. Hoed right alongside of him. Reckon when that tobacco got high enough to hide in, it could of told a heap of things went on besides hoeing. Looked like Rady and Annie enjoyed one another considerable. I've passed by late of an evening and seen them out there working together and they'd be laughing over something, the red high in Annie's cheeks and Rady's big shoulders dark with sweat bent over a hoe. He took to doing most of the chores around the place too. Fed the pigs for her, got in the night wood and water, mended the fences, kept the weeds out of the yard. And she took to cooking things he liked special to have on hand for him when he got hungry. Apple pie, and ham baked brown and crusty, and when the garden came on she kept tomatoes chilled for him by putting them in the spring house.

"She's a awful good cook," he told me one time.

And I said the thing that had been on my mind for some time. "You thinkin' of marryin' Annie, Rady?"

"I might," he said. "I might. That's a right nice farm she's got there."

But for all that, they never went anywheres together like folks courting. She went to meeting by herself, like always, and Lige walked her home. Rady never to say paid her any attention out any place. I don't think Annie liked that very much.

One night at meeting—I reckon it was the first time Rady

walked a girl home after his trade with Annie—he stepped up to Susie Bratton when the womenfolks filed out the door. Annie cut her eye at Rady and crimped her mouth. He didn't ever look at her. Just stepped off with Susie down the road and into the night. They had words about it the next day.

Annie was all bridled up when Rady went over to work in the tobacco. She never came out nor called to him when he cut through the yard on his way, and when good dark came on and he quit and went to the house she was setting on the porch, rocking. He set down and leaned up against a post and made himself a cigarette. "Lord," he said, "it shore is hot tonight. Brewin' up a storm, likely."

She never opened her mouth.

"Got the last of the crab grass out today," he said, drawing in a chest full of smoke. "Hit's a sight the way that stuff gits ahead of you if yer not keerful."

He could hear her chair squeaking as she rocked but she still never said a word. He rubbed his back against the post to scratch an itchy place. "Wisht I was down on the creek right now. I'd like to git cooled off."

"They's nothin' stoppin' you from goin'," Annie snapped at him then.

Rady looked over her way, surprised. "Now, what's the matter with *you*! What you got yore hackles riz up about?"

"I reckon you'd like to take that Susie Bratton swimmin' with you down there in the moonlight!"

"Now, listen, Annie . . ."

"You listen! Walkin' off with that little whore right in front of ever'body! Not a soul on the ridge but knows what you went fer! An' then you come over here as big as a gamecock! Struttin' around an' makin' me out a fool!"

Rady was struck speechless for a minute, and then he lashed out at her. "I've not come over here struttin' around like nothin'! I come over here, like always, to work that tobaccer patch! An' if you feel like a fool it's yer own doin', an' none of mine!"

She was crying by that time. It's a sad thing, but when a woman lets a man have his way with her she gives him the upper hand every time. She hands over to him the best that she's got, expecting him to cherish it, and he don't. She's got nothing left to work with, except tears when he don't do to suit her. And when the time comes she's got to weep, it's too late.

"Rady, you like that Susie Bratton?"

Rady went over and pulled her up out of the rocking chair and led her to the steps where he set her down and set down beside her. He put his arms around her and waited till she quit hiccuping. "Now, Annie, they's no need fer you cryin'. I don't like Susie Bratton an' you'd ort to know it. Fer that matter what if I got myself in a lather over Lige walkin' you home! Mebbe I don't like that!"

"But I jist keep goin' with Lige on account of folks mebbe talkin'. I can't hardly jist break off of a sudden. An' you know Lige ain't never . . . an' you an' Susie Bratton last night . . . an' I know you did . . . ."

Rady laughed at her real soft and snuggled her close up against him. She was a little woman, not to say fat, just a good armful. "You ain't got a thing to weary about if that's what's on yer mind," he said. "I never touched the girl. You think I would . . . after you?"

"I know good an' well you would!"

"Why, Annie!"

But she wanted to be persuaded. She wanted to believe he hadn't. "Rady? Didn't you?"

"I told you. I never touched her. Jist walked her home. An' only reason I done that was the same reason you let Lige come around. To keep folks from talkin'. I don't want nobody givin' you a bad name. An' I've allus walked a girl home now an' then, so it looked best to me to keep it up."

She was pacified then. She leaned against him, tired out, but at peace. "I never slept a wink last night," she said. "I was never so heavy-hearted in my life. Jist couldn't close my eyes fer thinkin'. Rady, you think a heap of me, don't you?"

No woman ought ever to ask a man that kind of question. There isn't but one answer he can give, she'd ought to know that. What peace does it bring a woman to ask a man if he loves her and know she's put the answer in his mouth. But they all do it.

"Shore," Rady said, just as quick as she'd of liked him to. "Shore, I think a heap of you. More'n anybody, fer that matter."

Like a kid that's been given a stick of candy she wiped her eyes and straightened up. "You want anything to eat?"

"Naw. Hit's too hot. I tell you, let's go swimmin' . . . me an' you!"

"Me? I can't swim, Rady. I'm skeered to death of water!"

"Well, you kin paddle around an' git cooled off while I swim, can't you? Moon's up an' hit'll be bright enough to see. Come on!"

Wanting to keep him sweet and tender like he was, wanting to stay happy with him again, wanting to convince herself this would last, she gave in, and like two kids, giggling, they set off down the holler to the creek.

The moon wasn't full but it was heavy towards it, and the sky was clean of clouds. Just a million stars dimmed by the moonlight, scattered like a hasty-spread pack of seeds. The creek lay like white ribbon in the night, and when they bent over it they could see theirselves give back, rippled and broken, but made whole when the waters stilled. Annie stepped out of her clothes, and her body looked white and cold in the moonlight, gleamy and shiny like a piece of china. Rady had never seen her so before, and he was struck with astonishment at how pretty she was formed. It was a false coldness the moon gave her, though, for Rady said Annie was always fire to touch, and fire to answer to . . . almost more than a man's own heat could match. She went towards him, dragging her feet in the sand, laughing at the way it squinched up between her toes. She pulled him down and then she laughed at the way the sand was warm on her back, and the way it tickled and was hard under her hips. Then she quit laughing.

Rady laid beside her, after, and he felt like she'd opened all the veins of his body and drained out the last drop of his blood. He remembered Susie Bratton and the night before. "God," he said, laughing, "I don't know what you want to weary about Susie Bratton for!"

Annie sat up and shook her hair down around her shoulders. "I jist don't want you touchin' nobody but me!" She turned around and gripped his arms. "Nobody but me, you hear, Rady Cromwell? You hear me?"

He slid his hands up under her hair. "I hear you. Nobody but you."

She pulled loose from him then and stood up, laughing again. "Come on.

Let's go swimmin'."

"I couldn't swim a stroke right now. I ain't got the strength to float, much less swim."

But she pulled at his hands and made him go in the water, and it was cool and clear and quiet.

When he took her home the moon was southing, and the fires were banked for the night.

Chapter Four

He made Annie a good crop tobacco and it brought a mighty fancy price when he took it off to market. A fancy price for those days. We'd never heard of parity then and seventeen-cent burley was damn good. That's what Rady got for his. And he split it with Annie. She was well pleased. "You done good as Harm," she told him, "ever' bit as good!"

"You're pleased?" he asked.

"I'm well pleased! Couldn't be no better pleased. I don't believe Lige'd of done anywheres near that good! Fer all yer jist a boy."

"Fer all I'm jist what?"

A slow blush commenced way down on Annie's throat and inched up over her face. "Well, in some ways . . . you know what I mean, Rady Cromwell! You ain't had the practice of makin' a crop on yer own, like a growed man would of, an' you've done good fer a start."

A start. That's the way he thought of it. And his mind was turning over several ways to go from there. I know he was thinking some of marrying Annie right off. We were shelling corn to take to the mill one morning when he spoke of it. His hands were broad and strong and they could strip an ear quicker than a rat. He kept busy while he talked, and the corn filled up in the bag. "I know I kin tend Annie's crop agin," he said, "but I'd ruther . . ."

"You'd ruther git yer hands on the whole thing, wouldn't you? That's what you'd ruther do!"

He threw a corn cob at me and laughed. "Well, why not? That's a right nice farm she's got. If I kin git it . . ."

He slid a red ear off to one side and picked up a white one. "I'd like to git aholt of them pastures, an' buy me up a dozen calves this fall to run on 'em. An' put in about fifteen more acres of corn."

"You got it all planned, ain't you? What does Annie have to say about it?"

"I've not to say . . . well, I've not exactly talked over all of it yit . . ."

"You've not said nothin' to her yit about marryin' her. Ain't that it?"

"Well, they ain't no use of raisin' the question till I know. I've heared some talk that Harm left a will that if she married agin she'll lose the farm. Some says his brother'll heir it if she marries agin."

"I've heared it too. But I disbelieve it. How many folks around here leaves a will that you know of?"

"That's a fact," Rady said. "Don't recollect nobody that ever did. But I'd shore like to find out. Wouldn't do me no good . . ."

"No, hit wouldn't," I said. "Whyn't you ask old Judge Morgan over at the county seat. He'd know."

"Reckon he'd tell?"

"Dunno. But he might. Wouldn't be no harm askin'. Worst he could do would be to tell you to git the hell out of his office."

We shelled a while without saying nothing and then Rady knotted the sack. "That's enough," he said and he pulled out a sack of Bull Durham and rolled him a cigarette. He handed me the sack and I shook out a paper full. "Rady," I said when I had the cigarette made an' lit, "would you like bein' married to Annie?"

He was leaning back against the side of the corn crib, his legs stretched out straight in front of him. "Would I like it how?"

"I mean . . . bein' married to her. Ain't she a awful lot older'n you?"

"What difference does that make?"

I never said anything.

"Shore I'd like bein' married to her," he went on after a time. "She's better'n ary kid I ever was with, if that's what you mean. But, hell, a man don't spend all his time in bed. Anyway, bein' married's jist about the same to anybody, ain't it? I ain't wearied none about that!"

"She's not never had no kids, has she?"

"No."

"You know why?"

"No, I ain't ever ast her."

"Reckon it's her can't have none?"

"Well, what if it is? Be a God's blessin', looks to me!"

"Don't you never want any young'uns?"

"Goddlemighty, how do I know? I've not never thought on it one way or another! I don't reckon anybody has 'em because they want 'em, do they? They jist come. Hit wouldn't frash me none if I never had ary one."

I picked up a corn shuck and commenced splitting it. "Twenty year from now she'd be in her fifties, wouldn't she? An' you'd jist be in yore thirties. Reckon how that would be?"

He raised himself up off the floor and heaved the sack of corn to his shoulder. "Twenty year from now I might be dead, too." He stepped down out of the corn crib and then he turned around to look at me. "Listen, kid. I'd marry my own grandma if I could better myself by so doin'. Don't weary yerself none about me an' Annie. The day you hear we're married, you kin figger I've done all right fer myself. An' that's all I aim ever to weary about. So don't lose no sleep over it."

Well, I'd said my say, and he'd said his. I could of just kept my mouth shut, for you never could argue Rady Cromwell out of nothing. Set in his ways, he was. Not to say stubborn. But just looking at things from all round, making up his mind and then not swerving.

So I went on home, and he went to the mill.

It was the next week, as best I can remember, Rady came by. "Go with me to the county seat," he said.

"What fer?"

"That's my business. Either go or stay, but no need to ast questions."

"Got ary thing to do with the law?"

"If you mean have I got to go to court, no! Dammit!"

I laughed and got my hat.

I knew well enough what he was going fer and I was right for when we got there he headed straight for Judge Morgan's office. The county seat is a little town built on a square around the courthouse, and the judge's office was on the first floor of the courthouse. I always liked to go in his office. It smelled like bourbon, law books and cigars. The judge had an old roll top desk over in one corner, and that's where he set mostly. In front of that desk. Brass spittoon set right handy to his swivel chair. The judge was a hefty man with ruffled white hair, and when you talked to him he puckered his mouth in at the corners and watched you over the tops of his bifocals. He looked up when we went in. "What kin I do fer you boys?" he said, right off.

Rady shifted his weight, but that was all the sign he gave that he was a mite nervous. "I'd like to ast a question, sir," he said, "a law question."

"Well, that's what I'm here fer. 'Course it might cost you to git a answer."

"Yessir. How much?"

"Depends on how much trouble it is. If I know it right off, it mightn't be but five dollars. If I got to look it up, then of course I got to have something fer my trouble. That's ten dollars, usually. If I got to go all over the place huntin' it down, it's liable to cost fifty dollars. Jist depends."

Rady got out his roll of bills. He had most of his tobacco money on him in cash. The judge commenced laughing. "Now, wait a minnit, young'un. Jist a common, ordinary question that I got right in my head, hit might be I wouldn't charge nothin' fer. Let's wait an' see."

Rady wadded the bills back in his pocket. "What I'd like to know, sir, is if a man is thinkin' of marryin' a woman, an' she's a widder an' got property, what happens when she gits married? To the property, I mean."

"I figgered that's what you meant," the judge said, kind of dry. "I allow I know what happens to the woman." He looked at Rady over his spectacles "You aimin' on gittin' married?"

"I'm thinkin' on it."

The judge aimed at the spittoon and hit it dead center. You could tell he'd had a heap of practice. "Yer thinkin' on it in case the widder's property goes with her. That it?"

Rady grinned and the judge shook his head. "Kind of a cold-blooded way to git married, seems to me. They ain't no romance left in you young squirts," he complained. "All you think of is gittin' yer hands on some widder's property."

"I don't mind gittin' my hands on the widder, too, Judge."

The judge took off his spectacles and polished them with a red bandanna handkerchief. "Well, now, that's nice. That eases my mind considerable. What kind of property is it? Real or personal?"

"Personal, I reckon. Hit belongs to her. It's real, too, though. Hit's a farm."

The judge puckered his mouth. "Nothin' much realer than a farm, is they?"

"No sir. I wouldn't say so."

"All right. What is it you want to know?"

"Hit's Harm Abbott's widder. I want to know if he left a will cuttin' her off should she git married agin. They's been talk he done so."

"What's yer name, boy?"

"Rady Cromwell."

"Old Preacher Cromwell's boy?"

"Yessir."

The judge stood up and laid his hand on Rady's shoulder. "I reckon you kin do with a little property, can't you? The widder's mite is allus welcome, be it for the good of the Lord or for the good of them raised in the fear of the Lord. No, he never left no will. I wish you well, son."

Yessir. How much I owe you?"

"Well, I reckon I kin give you that much advice free of charge. I tell you. Bein' an' old bachelor I'd like to go down in posterity. Jist name the first young'un after me."

"That's a deal," Rady grinned, and commenced backing out.

Outside, he looked at me and then he did a coon jig right in the middle of the street. "That's all I wanted to know," he said, "all I wanted to know!"

"You goin' to let me stand up with you at the weddin'?" I asked.

"Who else?" he said, clapping me on the back. "Who else?"

He'd made his mind up what to do. He went over to Annie's that very evening. Since the tobacco'd been through he hadn't had any excuse for going over there regular, so he'd been slipping off two or three times a week after dark. But he never waited for dark this day. He got there just before suppertime. Annie was taking a pie out of the oven and her face was pink and hot from the heat and the curls on the back of her neck were loose and damp. She straightened up when he came in, taking care not to jiggle her pie, and looked at him. "You must of knowed I was makin' custard pie," she laughed, "comin' jist at this time."

"No," he said, "but I'll git around to the pie. Put it down now. I want to talk to you."

She set the pie on the table and brushed her hair back from her forehead.

"Annie," he said, "let's git married."

She looked at him queer-like. "I must be hearin' things. Hit went to me like you said 'let's git married.'"

"That's what I said."

"When did you make up yore mind you wanted to git married?"

"I've allus wanted to."

"All the time?"

He nodded. "Right from the start. But it looked presumin'. Me with nothin'. But I got a little cash on hand now, an' I got a strong back. We git along real good, an' you got to have somebody tend yore place. Besides, I couldn't never look at another woman now."

She sat down in her little rocker and commenced crying. "I never thought to hear you say it! I've yearned fer it an' almost eat my heart out. But it never looked like you'd be wantin' to marry . . . well, I'm some older'n you, an' . . . well, I jist never thought it would come to pass."

He went over and sat down on the floor by her chair and put his head against her knee. "Annie," he said, gentle and soft, "Annie. I don't want you never agin to name bein' the oldest. I'm old fer my ways, an' you know what'll happen? You'll jist stand still an' I'll ketch up with you in no time at all! That's jist what'll happen. Jist wait an' see!"

To give him credit, he meant it. It didn't matter to him that Annie was might near double his years. And it wasn't hard for him to be gentle and sweet to her. He wasn't putting on nothing. He was fond of Annie. She had everything he wanted in a woman. She was good in bed and she had a good farm. Like he said, he'd of married his own grandma to better himself, and Annie was a sight better than his grandma. I reckon he'd of married Annie right then had she been another ten years older and as withered as a hag. He thought it was just his good luck and he was much obliged to her for being sightly like she was, and able to set him on fire to boot. The whole thing suited him fine.

She dried her eyes and got up to see to the pie. "You kin have a piece now. Hit's cooled sufficient," and she cut a quarter of it and slid it onto a plate for him.

"They's jist one thing, Annie," he said, swallowing a chunk of the pie down and talking around it, "I don't want no talk. I want this to be decent before ever'body. So I ain't comin' no more of a night. I ain't aimin' on touchin' you no more till we're married. I don't think they's been no talk up to now, an' I aim to see none commences."

He had a feeling of pride inside of him, times, that was downright funny in one so given to cutting corners and taking what he wanted as he pleased. He had that feeling now about getting married. Whatever his own reasons, he wanted it to look good in front of the settlement. He wanted it to be decent and proper.

Annie cut herself a piece of the pie and sat down across the table from him. She laughed a little at him then. "Ain't you thinkin' of the decencies a mite late?"

"In a way, yes. An' I'm sorry, Annie. Had I knowed, I'd never of touched you."

"Yer sorry?"

"I mean I'm sorry . . . well, we'd ort to of waited."

She came over and stood by him, leaning against him, letting her bosom lay soft and heavy against his cheek. "Yer sorry?" she said, whispering, and bending over him.

He laughed and grabbed her. "Jist oncet then. Jist oncet more, Annie."

They were lying on the bed, after. Annie was turned away from him and Rady was twisting one of the curls on her neck, thinking how soft it was and how nice her hair always smelled. He put his nose down on her neck and smelled again, and then he rolled close to her. "Annie," he said, "Annie. Let's get married soon."

It was dusky dark and the only light in the room was from the fire. It made red shadows across the bed and lit up their bodies. Made them look pale and melted. Rady looked at his own body, curved smooth and hard, and like copper in the firelight, his legs ropey and tough with young muscles. And he looked at Annie, whose skin gave off the fire like a piece of fine silk. All at once he felt too good to hold it. High and mighty . . . good. Clean and young and unbending strong. Like a bob-cat, crouched to spring, ready to rip. Wound up and tight-sprung, he was about to burst with the good way he felt, and he stretched long and touched the foot of the bed with his toes. "Let's git married soon," he said, "I want to git that hill pasture seeded come spring."

But he courted her proper for a month. Went to see her of a Sunday in broad daylight. Took the day with her. Walked her home from meeting of a Saturday night. And he made the old man loan him the team and wagon to take her to a quilting down at the far end of the ridge. He told the old man he was marrying Annie, and it was like he had stepped out from under and stood on his own feet. Now he was a man in his own right. Now he'd have a better farm than his pa. Now he could tell the old man, "I want the team today," and never say it asking. Just say it telling.

Annie thought that was a good time and place to give out the news. To settle it. She knew, being seen with Rady now, that they were talking. And wondering. So with all the womenfolks setting around the quilting frame she thought to tell them right out. She waited until the first of the gossip was laid by, and then she let it fall, like a stone in a still pond. And she set back and watched it ripple around the room. "Me an' Rady Cromwell is goin' to get married," she said.

Not bragging. Not even prideful. Just right. Just casual and level and careful. It's not good manners to brag. Each word separate and clean and unaccented, she said it. They made out to be surprised, which was right. There was a hum and a buzz. "You an' Rady Cromwell!" they said. "Why, we thought Lige Sherman was . . . well, we thought you an' Lige . . . well . . . well, now ain't that nice? Rady is a awful good boy. He'll allus do good, Annie. He's jist plumb clever. But you shore pulled the wool over our eyes! You shore put one over on us!" Like they hadn't mouthed it up and down the ridge from the first time he took her home from meeting. But being mannerly to the last.

Annie let it go on a time. Behind their words she knew what they were thinking. She knew what the slanted looks meant. She knew they would talk different when she was gone. Knew they'd be saying, "Well, I never! Oh, I knowed they was somethin' up! Well, upon my word an' honor! Her an' Rady Cromwell! An' her old enough to be his ma! Who would have dreamt Rady Cromwell . . ." and then with a shrug, "he's smart, that Rady. She's got a real good farm!" Oh, she knew.

She let the talk run along and then she stepped in and took it over. "Lige is a nice man," she said, thoughtfully, considerately. "But he's gittin' on in years." She did it on purpose. Lige was no older than their men, and well she knew it. He was no older than Harm had been, but she had to pay them off for what they were thinking, and for what they had not said, but would say when she was gone. "But Rady . . ." and she laughed sweetly, knowing how quickly the vision of him would spring before them, young, strong and hickory-stout, like their own sons . . . and they, withered with bearing sons, wrinkled and old, while she, passed by, kept her bloom . . . "but Rady," she said, and looking around the room she took all of them into the sweet mystery of Rady, "Rady is so strong-headed. He jist . . . well, he jist swept me off my feet!"

Bitterly they listened, gall flowing beneath their tongues.

When had a man looked at them with favoring eyes! When had they been swept off their feet, if ever! When had any man, save the broken and shambled one that slept in their beds, laid a hand on a one of them! And their envy was green and acid. "I reckon," she went on innocently, "I reckon we'll git married on Valentine's Day."

They nodded their heads. "Hit's a good day fer a weddin'. Where you aimin' on gettin' married?"

"We're aimin' on havin' a real nice weddin'. We ain't goin' to the county seat an' stand up before the judge nor nothin' like that. We're aimin' on gittin' the preacher to come an' have it at my house. I'd like you all to come."

So on Valentine's Day they were married. In the fireplace room at Annie's house. Annie wore a new flowered silk dress she'd ordered from the mail order and Rady wore a new blue suit he'd got in town. They looked fine and handsome standing up there in front of the preacher and the folks. But being the one to stand up with him, I was close enough I could see the beads of sweat break out on Rady's forehead during the ceremony. It makes any man break out in a sweat to stand up in front of a bunch of folks and get married. I don't know why. Most time he's doing what he wants to do, of his own free will. But right at the last minute, when there's no backing out of it, when he's roped and hogtied and no getting loose, he gets shaky and unsure. I like to of sweated clean through my coat the day I got married. And getting married was what I wanted to do the worst way. But outside of sweating a little Rady didn't show a thing and his hands never had a tremor when he put the ring on Annie's finger.

I've not been to many weddings but what few I've been to it always seemed to me there was an awkward time the first minute or two when the preacher got done. Like neither the bride nor the groom or the folks present know quite what to do. But when the preacher said the last amen, Rady turned real quick to Annie put his arms around her and kissed her hard, just like nobody else was there. He never hurried a bit. It was like he wanted them all to see he couldn't wait. Like he meant them to know he was crazy about her and proud she was marrying him. And when he'd finished kissing her and they turned around to face the folks he kept his arm around her waist all during the handshaking and well-wishing. Like he couldn't stand not touching her every minute of the time. I don't know how much of it was that queer streak of pride in him and how much of it was real. But I reckon it was a pretty good mixture of both. Anyhow, like Annie the day of the quilting, he took his own way of denying he was marrying a farm instead of a woman.

We shivareed them that night. And man, it was a fine one! When we shivaree a couple back here in the hills we wrap it up good! That night we had shotguns, cowbells, dishpans, old iron bars, anything at all that would make a noise. During the wedding dinner a couple of us had sneaked into the bedroom and hung a cowbell under the bed. We'd tied a cord to it and run it though a hole under the window. So we crept up right easy-like that night and aimed to commence the shivaree by pulling stout on that cord to the cowbell. We figured they'd be in bed where any newly-wed couple had ought to be on their wedding night. I was the one got my hand on the cord first, and I got all set and give it a mighty yank! It come loose free in my hand and next thing I knew I was turning a couple of somersets backwards from the strength of my haul. There I laid, like a complete idiot! The breath knocked plumb out of me! I'd ought to of known you couldn't put nothing over on Rady Cromwell!

Well, then somebody gave the signal and we commenced our noise. All those shotguns firing, all those dishpans banging, all the cowbells ringing and all the shouting and screeching and yelling! It liked to of jarred the hills loose from their foundations! Rady and Annie came out on the porch right away. Never kept us waiting hardly any time. They came out holding hands and laughing kind of sheepish-like. I don't reckon there's ever a time in a man's life when he feels as good and at the same time as much of a damn fool as at his own shivaree. Kind of proud and kind of ashamed. There's not much left to the imagination, for a fact. The whole thing is aimed and pointed at the joining of a man and a woman, and the jokes get pretty rugged and some of the action is not very misleading. But Rady and Annie took it right good.

The womenfolks made a dive for Annie and pulled her off the porch and dumped her into a big washtub and hauled her around the house three or four times, laughing and going on with some fancy screeching and yelling. And we got a rail off the fence and hoisted Rady. "Now take it easy, boys," he said, laughing, "you wouldn't want to cripple me! Not on my weddin' night, anyways!"

I was standing next him and to save my life I couldn't help looking up at him and grinning. He winked. "Was you the son of a gun put that cowbell under the bed?"

"How'd you happen to find it?"

"Looked fer it, of course. Have you fergot I tied one under yore's an' Junie's bed?"

I had. Plumb forgot it was Rady. No wonder he'd thought of it. Me, I hadn't. And Junie never did get over that. Like it was my fault! But I must admit it was right startling.

When all the shooting and shouting was over we poured into the house and ate the rest of the wedding dinner. Rady had fixed for the shivaree by getting in two or three jugs of moonshine and Uncle Jett had brought his fiddle. We had us a time! Annie never held with dancing regular, it being against her religion, but a shivaree is kind of special, so she gave in and danced the first set with Rady. Wasn't much room for nobody to dance, though, so mostly we just milled around. Rady was leaning up against the wall alongside of me at the last, and if the room was spinning as fast for him as it was for me he had good reason to stand propped up! He was watching the folks and he had a kind of easy, good-natured grin on his face.

"Ever'thing goin' to suit you?" I asked him.

"Ever'thing," he said, straightening up. "Today I got me a woman, an' I'm eighteen year old. Hit suits me jist fine!"

"Is Valentine's Day yore birthday?"

He nodded. "One reason we picked it."

I was just hazy enough to say a thing was on my mind. "You taken the brown girl, didn't you, Rady?"

He puckered his brow.

"You know," I said, "in the song . . . the brown girl had the house an' land."

He grinned then. "Yeah. But they ain't no fair Elinore!"

The duties of a host claimed him then and he left me to the problem of my own propping. One more drink out of the jug, though, and it wasn't a problem any more. That wall just folded up behind me and I laid my head against it like it was a pillow and went to sleep. That was some shivaree!

Chapter Five

So Rady and old Drum and his gittar moved over to Annie's. And he lost no time going over his new farm. It must of felt good to him to have his own place. There's nothing like reaching down and picking up a handful of the earth, crumbling it between your fingers, smelling it and even tasting it and knowing it's your own. This little patch of dirt, weedy, scrubby, even rocky, is what's yours of the whole wide world. You can stand strong on it because it belongs to you. You can plant yourself and take root, and grow bigger and stouter because of it. No matter what you ever own in the way of property and things, it's the ownership of land that is the final and best ownership. For there's a kinship between a man and his land that don't hold true with other things. Maybe it's the knowing that in the end you go back to it . . . maybe it's the knowing that somehow, some place, you come from it . . . maybe it's the power you've got over it to make it birth something you need . . . maybe it's just the knowing that with all your power over it, it has the last power over you, for without land there's nothing.

Whatever it is, if a man's been raised on the land, if he's worked it and cursed it and blessed it, he belongs to it and it to him and there's no parting the two. Even when he curses it, he'll walk across it prouder for owning it, and when he blesses it, it's like something fine and giving had been poured into him. It's a wondrous thing to own a piece of land. And Rady was learning now what it was like. He had come now to the fourth thing he loved . . . land, and a man's power over it. For Annie had told him that night it was all his. Of her own free will, without him asking, she'd offered it. "I want it should be that way," she'd said. Lawfully it would of come to him anyways, I reckon, but it made it a heap better for her to be trusting of him. "I've got no misdoubts about it, Rady," she'd said. "You'll take keer of the land, an' you'll take keer of us." A woman can find no prouder words than that to say to the man she's picked.

"You kin put yer dependence on it," Rady promised her, "I'll do good with it."

The place set on a little knoll that was grown over with tall grass and fine trees, big, high-standing beech and walnut trees, and the front rolled down the pasture to a sweet spring in the beginnings of the holler. An old rail fence followed the curve of the knoll and hemmed in the house, which was weathered and gray, but build solid in its time. It was built like most ridge houses, in the shape of a "T". Two rooms and a hall in front, with two rooms in the ell behind. It had a big, roomy porch clean across the front, and a nice, screened work porch in the back. Big enough, stout enough and good enough for Rady and Annie.

Annie bloomed like a full grown rose those first days after they were married. Happiness and the knowing she's loved does a heap for a woman. For any woman. But it was like a tonic for Annie, at her age. She sung as she worked and she swept up and kept her house shining, and she cooked like Rady was a dozen hungry men. Nothing was too good for him. I was there at suppertime one evening. "Jist come eat with us," Rady said, when she called him in.

"No, I better be gittin' on back home."

"They ain't no use of that. Come taste Annie's vittles. You don't know what good eatin' is till you've eat Annie's cookin'. Come on."

I let myself be talked into it and set down to table with them. I recollect there was ham and hot biscuits and baked sweet potatoes and tomato preserves and cucumber pickles. And beans cooked tender and soupy. There was pie, too. Like a Sunday dinner it was. "My God, Annie," I said, "you'll git Rady so fat he can't stoop over to do a lick of work! You feed him like this all the time?"

"All the time!" Rady said, proud-like.

"A man works as hard as Rady needs plenty of good, strengthenin' food," Annie said. "I aim to see he gits it."

We eat and then Rady and me went in the fireplace room to set whilst Annie did up the dishes. The talk went one way and another, like it does when two men come together. Rady had big plans. "With the money the two of us has got," he said, "I kin easy seed that new field an' buy me ten or twelve calves. I ain't aimin' to put my dependence in tobaccer by itself. They's money to be made in beef stock, an' I've been wantin' to try my hand at it. An' I mean to git Annie another cow or two so's she kin sell the cream. A man had ort to have out several strings, seems to me."

It sounded mighty fine and I was pleased for him. I had a notion he'd do just about what he said he would. Most of us on the ridge farm our thirty or forty acres kind of easy come, easy go. I, for one, like the feel of a fishing pole in my hands on a hot July day better than a hoe and I've never noticed but what the tobacco grew just about as fast as the weeds, or a little faster. I've not never been one to frash myself when it come to hard work, not being beset by any noticeable ambitions along that line. But Rady was cut of a different stripe, and I knew in reason he'd set himself a goal and would hump right along until he got where he'd aimed to go.

So I wasn't surprised but precious little when fall come around that year and he had him a fine pasture seeded, with around a dozen head of calves fattening on it. He'd got Annie a couple more milk cows and she was getting a right smart cream check every week. He had some fine-looking pigs on the side, too. He put a new roof on the barn and built a shed room on both sides so's it'd house his new cows, cleared a woods tract Harm'd never got around to and put it in corn, and he had fine tobacco and corn both that year. Him and Annie were in a good way to better themselves. Annie worked right alongside of him and made the most of everything he did. She was a good woman to help. Stout and able to keep up.

And him and Annie made out all right with one another too. Had Annie been a bearing woman I've no doubts a young'un would of commenced showing right off. The womenfolks kept their eye on her anyways, not knowing but what it had been Harm at fault the first time. But they kind of relaxed their watch when time went by and Annie's dresses never showed no signs of hiking up in front. They clucked their tongues and shook their heads and said what a pity, but most would of give a year's tobacco money to pass two years hand-going without another young'un dragging at them. Most nursed their latest one a sight longer than was needed, to keep their health from coming back on them to get them in the family way again. It was just one more thing that Annie was lucky in, had they owned up to their rightful feelings.

Junie didn't make no bones about wishing she had it easy like Annie. But I don't know. Believe I'd rather have too many as none at all. Of course four kids in four years is kind of hard on a woman. I know, but I can't rightly see as what's to be done about it if she's quick to take.

Outside of working pretty hard Rady was about the same as always. Went coon hunting and fox hunting with the rest of us, and he still tilted the jug when he was a mind to. Still took a turn in the bushes with Susie Bratton or whoever was handy when he wanted. Never was a ridge man yet felt a wedding ceremony put an end to his natural pleasures. Just made him have to take a little more care. No man wants to have trouble with his woman, but he'd feel a fool if he passed up a good chance for a roll in the hay. And Rady was no exception.

Come September of the second year they were married and I went by one evening to get him to go squirrel hunting. He'd been cutting tobacco. Little later than most, but he had a big crop out and was just winding it up. He was cleaning the tobacco gum off his hands with turpentine when I went around the corner of the house. "Git yer gun," I told him. "Let's git us some squirrels. I'm aimin' on sinkin' my teeth in a mess of fried squirrels fer breakfast in the mornin'."

He looked up, his eyes squinted against the turpentine fumes. "Now, I take right kindly to that idee," he said. "Wait'll I get my hands clean."

"You been?" I asked him.

He shook his head. "Nary a time. Too busy in the tobaccer."

I leaned my gun up against the wall and rolled me a cigarette. "You've heared," I said, "what all work an' no play does to man!"

He scoured soap on his hands and laughed. "I've heared. An' I believe it. Be right nice to draw a bead on a squirrel fer a change."

Annie had come to the door. She'd heard us talking. "You want to eat before you go?"

"A snack," he says. "Don't want to waste the daylight."

She fixed us a little something to eat and we pulled out. Went down the holler and across the draw and circled around through his woods. Had good luck, too. First thing we found several hickory trees where the squirrels had been and we just set down and waited. It was a still evening, no wind through the leaves, the light fading but still good. Directly a fox squirrel came peeping around a high limb. Rady nudged me, but I nodded for him to take it. Facts is, he was a little too far for me and I'd of missed him. Rady drew a bead on it, waited a minute and cut loose. The squirrel toppled fifty foot to the ground. Right through the eye! Man, that guy could shoot! I'm pretty good, but I couldn't of hit that one, and I've been known to put a slug in the back a time or two. But if Rady ever did he never told it, and I sure never saw him do it!

We moseyed on and I got me one, and then for about an hour while the light held we found several all the way down the holler. Got us five or six apiece. "That's aplenty," Rady said, finally. "Gittin' too dark to see."

"Yeah," I said, "jist a waste of shell to keep on. This'll make a good mess, anyways."

We angled through the woods towards the road and climbed over the rail fence at the place where Rady's farm joined onto the Del Hall place. Rady looked at the fence as we climbed over and shook his head. "I got to put a new fence in here," he said. "This'n has been here since time begun an' it's jist about to rot down."

"Them woods'd be a good place to run yer hogs," I said, "if you'd git you a good fence here."

"Yeah. That's what I been thinkin'."

We went on down the road past the Hall place. The Del Hall place was probably the best property in these parts. Old Man Hall had come to New Ridge from some place in Indiana, back twenty, thirty years ago. He'd bought this place and improved it a heap. Added to it until he had around a couple of hundred acres. Had good buildings, a nice house, and a fine farm. Was the only place in our parts had lights and water. He'd put in one of those Delco systems. It was sure enough a place to make a man's mouth water.

It was just getting first dark as we went past, but we could make out Old Man Hall himself leaning on the gate. We spoke. "Howdy, boys," he said. "Any luck?"

Rady held up his bag of squirrels and I held up mine. Old Man Hall eyed them. "Not bad," he said. "Not bad. Right nice little mess."

"Never went till late," Rady told him, "an' the light got bad right away. They's plenty this year."

"That's what I been hearin'. Got to git me a mess 'fore I leave."

"You goin' somewheres?" I asked.

The old man propped his foot against the cross bar of the gate. "I've sold the place," he said, running his hand down the top rail that was smooth as satin from the years. "Mama an' me's goin' back to Indianny."

Well, that took both Rady and me all of a heap! Sell a fine place like this one! We couldn't understand it, but the old man went on to explain. "The boys is all married an' gone, an' me an' Mama are gittin' too old to work as hard as we been. We thought we'd jist sell out an' take it easy fer a time."

"Who bought the place?" Rady asked.

"Feller by the name of Rowe. City feller. Lives somewheres in the east. From the looks of him I don't figger he's much of a farmer, but that ain't none of my put-in. Claimed he wanted to live in the country."

"He shore picked the country!" I said.

The old man laughed. "He did that!"

"When you leavin'?" Rady said.

"I got to give possession in thirty days. Reckon we'll git gone next week or two. He'll need a little time to git hisself moved in."

"Buy ever'thing?" Rady said.

"Lock, stock an' barrel."

"Well, I shore hate to see you go," I says. "New Ridge won't seem the same without you folks."

He was rubbing at the top rail yet, and he said right slow-like, "Hit'll go quare to me to give it up," and then he kind of squared his shoulders up. "But hit's best, I reckon. Mama is set on it, leastways."

Rady hitched his gun around. "Well, we'd best be gittin' on. Jist go up with us, Mister Hall."

"Guess I'd better stay here," the old man said, turning back towards the house. "You boys be good neighbors with Mister Rowe."

"We'll do that," we promised, and we took off up the road.

Rady turned around at the bend in the road and looked back. He looked a long time. You could just make out the house and the buildings in the dusky light, and they set white and sweet against the sky, the trees banked back of them. "God, that's a pretty place," Rady said. "Pretty as a picture! I'd shore love to have it."

"Who wouldn't?" I snorted. And then, for what reason I don't know, I said. "Annie can't help you git that place, Rady."

He looked at me and grinned. "No. I don't reckon she kin at that." He looked once more at the house and barns and then turned up the road again. "But I'd love to have it jist the same."

"You got a nice place," I told him. "An' all you kin tend."

"A man don't never have mor'n he kin tend," he said. He stopped and made water in the road and I remember the dust raised in little puffs and settled back down, heavy and cloudy. And I laughed. "Rady, you got too big a appetite."

"Mebbe," he said, buttoning up. "But they ain't nothin' wrong with my digestion."

The Halls left the ridge in a couple of weeks and the next thing we knew the Rowes had moved in. It was a seven days' wonder the stuff they brought. Had everybody on the ridge marveling. A piano, fancy furniture, barrels and barrels of dishes, big fine rugs and pictures and things. Was four moving vans brought the stuff, and while the Hall place was a big old house, it must of crowded it some to get it all inside. The Rowes never came with their stuff. The moving men said they were coming down later. And for several days the house just set there, furniture and boxes every which way, and the shades pulled down plumb to the sill.

We never knew exactly when they came. One day the house was setting there, nobody around, and the next the shades were up and folks were stirring. They had a woman and man to do for them until they got settled in. It went queer, but we all reckoned they had money and must be used to being waited on.

For a week I'd say there were curtains and things on the clotheslines in the yard, blowing in the wind, and rugs on the fences airing, and a big to-do generally. And then one of the womenfolks said they saw her riding hell-for-leather down the road one evening just at good dark, like something was chasing her. Said they knew it was her on account of her black hair. The way news leaks around the ridge it hadn't taken folks long to know it was Miz Rowe had the long, black hair. So when they saw this woman riding a big chestnut horse, running him like the wind, and her hair streaming out behind her, they knew it was her. It gave everybody kind of a shiver, for the ridge women don't ride like that. Don't ride at all if there's any help. And at best it's usually an old work mule with a sidesaddle, or just a blanket thrown over.

"Well, a woman's got a right to ride her own horse if she wants to," I told Junie. "They ain't nothin' wrong with that."

"No," she sniffed, her nose up in the air, "they ain't nothin' wrong with it. But you mark my words! They's somethin' quare up at that big house. Somethin' almighty strange an 'quare. They ain't nothin' wrong with a woman ridin' her own horse, like you say. But she wasn't ridin' accordin' to what they say. She was runnin' that horse like they was a devil after her, a-layin' all bent over its neck, that black hair of her'n streamin' out behind her, like a devil herself. They ain't our kind of folks, an' you kin jist put it down I've said so!"

"Wasn't nobody ever said they was our kind of folks," I says.

"I don't recollect but what we've allus knowed they was rich folks an' would be different. Hit bein' our first time around folks like that, of course things is goin' to seem quare. But they've bought the place an' we're beholdin' to be neighborly."

"Neighborly! How kin you neighbor with a wild woman!"

"Now, Junie . . ."

"Set down there an' eat yer supper! An' leave the neighborin' to me! Menfolks'll allus excuse a good-lookin' woman!"

"Is she good-lookin'?"

As innocent as I made that remark Junie pounced on it. "As if you never knowed!"

"I've not laid eyes on her!" I swore, between a mouthful of meat and potatoes.

"Well, that ain't because you ain't tried! You've been past there a dozen times since they moved in!"

"The road runs right by," I said.

"An' I don't recollect you've ever loped it so steady, neither!"

"Now, Junie . . ."

"Oh, shet up!"

And I did so, seeing right then the peace of the settlement was as good as gone for the time being. That black-haired woman was going to be a thorn in the flesh to the women of the ridge. And a man with as much mind as a goose would take heed mighty quick not to give his woman reason to rile up. Junie being like she was, I knew in reason not to give her an argument then, nor never. And I knew, also, I'd best be commencing to take care.

It was Rady, though, got the first glimpse of Mister Rowe. He was putting in that new fence on the line between the places and he was making a clatter with the posthole diggers and didn't hear him nor see him until he was right up on him. Mister Rowe was riding a neat little black mare. He spoke first, of course, "Hello, there. You must be my new neighbor."

Rady clacked the diggers together and lifted out the dirt and released it. Then he laid the diggers down and wiped his forehead. "Yes, sir," he said, walking over towards the man, "though I'd say it was *you* was *my* new neighbor. I was here first," and he laughed and put out his hand. "My name's Rady Cromwell."

Mister Rowe got down off his horse and stuck out his hand. He was a taller man than Rady, built on the slight side, almost thin, but awful handsome. Had a kind of white skin and real black hair. Had black eyes to go with it and a soft, womanish-looking mouth. Rady was taken by surprise on account of him being so much younger than he'd expected. He wasn't more than thirty, I'd reckon. "My name's Rowe," he said. "You're right about me being the new neighbor, though. Putting up a new fence?" he said.

It's a funny thing how folks from outside go around saying things don't need saying. Anybody could see Rady was digging postholes and there was a roll of hog wire laying on the ground in plain sight. If Mister Rowe had wanted to say something about the fence he could of asked Rady if he'd struck rock digging the holes, or if he was going to use cedar or locust posts. But Rady was polite. "Yes, sir," he said, "they've not been gone over fer several years, an' I'm aimin' on turnin' my hogs loose in the woods. Don't want 'em gittin' out an' runnin' over yore land."

Mister Rowe laughed. "No, I don't suppose that would do." He had a twitchy way of pulling at his lower lip. He tugged at it with two fingers and pinched it together. It made his mouth look puckered and narrow. "This is as far as my place goes, isn't it?"

"Yes, sir. This is the line between my place an' yore'n."

Mister Rowe kept pinching his mouth and he stared off in the woods. "I'm trying to find a good tenant," he said directly. "You know anybody I could get? I can't take care of this big place by myself."

"You got no kids?"

Mister Rowe laughed again. "No."

Rady pushed his hat back on his head and scratched his forehead where his hat band had left a mark. "Well, it's a awful big place fer a man to try to work by hisself. Young'uns come in handy on a place this size. Mister Hall's renter ain't goin' to stay on?"

"No. He's bought a place of his own."

Rady studied. "Hit's gittin' pretty late in the season to be lookin' fer a renter," he said finally. "Most has done been contracted."

"I know. But I've got to find someone. Matter of fact, Cromwell, I'm no farmer at all. Never farmed in my life."

Now Rady had his own kind of gall, so he just come right out and asked what was on his mind, unmannerly though it was. "How come you to buy this place if you ain't no farmer? Old Man Hall was a good farmer. An' hit'll take good farmin' to keep it up."

Mister Rowe kind of drew back in himself like Rady had ventured too far, and then he seemed to think better of it. "The fact is," he said, kind of slow-like, "I'm not very well. I've been ill, and we bought this place so I could live quietly in the country and rest and recuperate. But I can't afford not to make it pay. I'll tell you, Cromwell," and it was like he'd made up his mind of a sudden, "I spent almost the last dime I had to buy this place, and I've got to make it pay. But I'll have to have a good tenant."

"What kind of a deal you got?" Rady asked.

"Deal?"

"Deal. Trade. Proposition. What you goin' to offer?"

"What's usual around here?"

Rady was almost plumb disgusted with him, and he couldn't help wondering what the fool was going to come to. But he told him. "A third's usual," he said, "an ever'thing furnished."

Mister Rowe frowned. "What does that mean? Everything furnished?"

"Hit means you furnish a man a place to live, the land, the tools, the teams an' feed fer 'em, the seed, the fertilizer . . . ever'thing. A tenant don't put out nothin' but his time. But you got a call on that six days a week from daylight till dark."

"That seems like a hell of a lot to furnish! And then he gets a third of the profits?"

"That's right. "That's the way of it."

"Would a man like that take enough interest to keep the place up?"

Rady shrugged. "Depends on who you git. Some would. Some'd see it as a good chancet to git a start. An' then they's some wouldn't give a damn. Some'd have to be watched ever' minnit."

"Can you recommend someone?"

Rady studied a minute. "Not jist offhand. Like I said, hit's gittin' late in the season to be closin' up with a man. I can't think of nobody right off. But I'll keep it in mind."

Mister Rowe thanked him and got back on his horse. He could sure sit a horse now. Looked like he'd been born on a horse the way he rode. Slim and easy and loose. "I'll be grateful for any suggestions, Cromwell," he said, turning the mare. "I'm almost helpless here."

Rady picked up his posthole diggers and grinned to himself. Brother, you shore are, he thought.

Mister Rowe turned back after he'd started off. "Oh yes. You know a good bootlegger close by?"

"You ever drunk moonshine, Mister Rowe?"

The man laughed down at Rady. "No. But I guess I'll learn."

Rady spoke kind of dry then. "You got quite a lesson to learn, I'd say. I'll send you a man over."

"Thanks," and this time Mister Rowe kept going.

Rady told Annie about it that night. "Why, the biggity thing," she said, surprised at anybody being so unthoughtful and stuck-up. "Why, I was jist fixin' to go over to see his woman the next day or two! I was jist aimin' on takin' her a hot apple pie an' goin' to see if they was ary thing I could do to help her git settled."

"I wouldn't," Rady said. Supper was over and Annie was redding up the dishes and Rady was smoking whilst watching her. He had his chair propped against the wall. "From what I could tell, they ain't used to this country, an' doubtless they've got quare ways from us. You'd ort to of heared him talk . . . proper!" And Rady laughed at the remembrance of how proper Mister Rowe made his words. "Like a perfessor," he said, "jist so . . ." and he mocked Mister Rowe's way of talking. ". . . 'I'd be grateful for any suggestions, Cromwell,' *Cromwell!* Jist like I was a field hand!"

Annie jerked the dishrag in the water. "I declare! Hit does look like a body would of had the manners to say Rady or Mister Cromwell, if he was a mind to use yer last name! An' us havin' to live neighbors with 'em! I was hopin' they'd be real nice folks like the Halls. You goin' to say more to him about a renter?"

"Well, hit wouldn't hurt none I reckon. I'll study on it."

"I heared the Pringles was lookin' fer a place."

"I thought they was tied up with Old Man Crewel."

"Not the way I heared it. They's some dissatisfaction. The Pringles has got enough kids that they could tend that big place, I reckon."

"Yeah. Got three or four boys, ain't they?"

"Three. Nigh growed. An' the girls is comin' on, too. They's two of them as best I recollect."

"Well, I might name 'em to Mister Rowe. Wouldn't hurt none, noways."

He let his chair hit the floor and stood up and dumped his pipe out on the apron of the stove. He put the pipe on the table and walked over to Annie and slid both arms around her. "Ain't you done washin' them dishes yit?"

Annie leaned back against him and looked up at him. "Soon."

"Yer drippin' dishwater all over with that rag. Come on."

Annie slung the dishrag back in the water. "My sakes, what a mess! Let me go, Rady. I'll git the mop."

But Rady just tightened his arms around her and rubbed his face against her hair. Sleepy-like she closed her eyes and put her arms about his neck. "Clean it up after," Rady said, and he turned her around towards the bedroom. "I been waitin' more'n a hour already fer you to git done with them measly dishes. That's too long."

"Rady!" she said, acting like she never wanted to go. But she didn't really mind. And she went. Funny how a woman likes to have a man act masterful. Especially when he wants her. Reckon there's something about it makes her feel like what she's giving is a bigger gift that way. Or maybe it's that they like for it to be taken. The feeling of being helpless maybe takes away any need for shame. I misdoubt there ever was a woman didn't feel a kind of sin with a man. Even when it's a nice, legal sin. Or maybe it's the sin makes it nice. Not being a woman, I wouldn't know. But I've thought on it.

It rained for a week or more then before Rady could go back to fencing. First day it faired up though he was back digging postholes, and he hadn't been at it more'n an hour until Mister

Rowe came trotting over, on foot this time. "God, Cromwell," he said, "I'm about perished! I've got to find someone right away. Have you thought of anybody?"

"Well, they's jist one family don't seem to be tied up yit. The Pringles over in the creek bottom. They been sharin' fer Old Man Crewel over there, two or three years. But my wife tells me they's some dissatisfaction an' they're lookin' fer another place. I don't know what's back of them wantin' to move on . . . may be them at fault . . . may be old man Crewel. An' I don't know a heap about 'em, except they've got the name of workin' good. I know they's a big family of 'em, an' that's allus a help tendin' a big place. You might go over an' talk to the old man an' see would he consider movin' here."

"You think they could take care of the place?"

"Well, they *could*. They ain't no doubts about that. But they ain't no renter goin' to tend a place right without he's told what to do. You'll have to keep aholt of the reins yerself."

"Yes. I see."

"What about that man an' woman you got workin' fer you now? Couldn't they help around the place?"

"They aren't my . . . well, they live in the East. They just came with us temporarily. They'll be leaving shortly."

Nothing was said for a time and then Rady said, "The man come with yer moonshine?"

Mister Rowe acted like he was gagging, "Christ, yes! What does he make? Liquid lightning?"

Rady grinned. "I tried to tell you."

"Nobody could tell you! The lining of my throat was scorched for a week! But it packs a mean wallop, doesn't it?"

"Yessir. Right smart of a wallop. But you'll git to where you won't touch nothin' else after you been drinkin' it a while. Regular whiskey'll taste like swamp water to you. Hit don't take much to do a feller, neither."

"I found that out! I was too drunk to find the bed after a couple of good snorts."

"Must of been right good ones then. They's men hereabouts drinks a quart a day, year in an' year out. Think nothin' of it."

"I'll have to work up to that. Where'll I find these Pringles?"

"Go down Old Ridge to the pike, follow it two, three miles an' turn off down a dirt road on the right. Hit leads to Old Man Crewel's place. They live in the house jist this side the main house."

Mister Rowe pulled at his mouth and Rady noticed his hands were shaky. He figured those two snorts must of been awful big ones, for two drinks won't leave a man quivering the next day. He reckoned, too, that Mister Rowe must be a pretty hard-drinking man, on account of him asking so quick for a bootlegger.

Then seemed like Mister Rowe made up his mind about something. "Come on over to the house and have a drink, Cromwell."

Rady looked down at his boots and his muddy overhalls. "I'm pretty mucky, Mister Rowe, to be goin' in somewheres."

"Oh, that doesn't matter. Come on."

So they went to the house and Mister Rowe took Rady in through the kitchen door and led him on into the front room. Leastways it had been the front room when the Halls lived there. Mister Rowe had fixed it into something else. One of those dens or studies you see in the pictures in magazines. There were books clean to the ceilings all around and a piano . . . one of those baby grands. He had a swell big gun cabinet along one wall and a heap of pretty guns racked there. Rady noticed them first, of course, and he couldn't help going over and looking closer.

"Like guns?" Mister Rowe said.

"Crazy about 'em," Rady said. "But I've not seen any this fine before."

Mister Rowe went over and unlocked the glass door and flung it back. "Handle them," he said. "See what you think of them."

There must of been twelve or fifteen of the finest guns made, shotguns of every gauge, and high-powered rifles of all kinds. Rady had never seen the like and he took hold of each one as delicate as if it'd been a baby. "Man, man," he said, fondling them.

"Ever do any big game hunting?" Mister Rowe asked him.

"No, sir. Nothin' bigger'n foxes an' coons."

"Foxes around here?" Mister Rowe perked right up.

"Thousands of 'em. Pests an' nuisances. Can't hardly keep fowls on account of 'em."

Mister Rowe had poured each of them a drink and he handed a glass to Rady. "I've never done any fox hunting. Hunted bear and deer, elk and goat, but never have tried fox hunting. By God, that might make living down here fairly interesting! Can you take me some time?"

"Any time. I got a pretty good hound, an' we kin take a night any time you say."

"That's a promise, Cromwell, I'm going to hold you to it."

"All right by me, sir."

You couldn't help saying sir to Mister Rowe. He held himself so straight and proud, talked so proper and right, and was so easy and smooth in his ways. You had to figure him for a man that'd always been used to nice things and nice ways of living. And the sir slipped out in spite of yourself. It kind of went with the man.

Rady took his drink down. "That's mighty smooth likker, Mister Rowe."

"That's bonded. The last I've got. And I can't afford any more." He laughed, kind of dry and bitter. "It'll be the local brand from here on out."

"You'll git used to it," Rady said.

"Yes." Then he laughed.

Rady noticed a cabinet over in the corner and a lot of records stacked by it. He wandered over and looked at them. "Is this a victrola?" he asked.

"A phonograph, yes."

"You shore got a lot of records."

"Quite a few. Do you like music?"

"Yessir. But I don't know nothin' much about it. I got me a gittar an' I pick it some."

Mister Rowe filled their glasses again. He held his up to the light and studied it. "Well, here's to your gittar, Cromwell. May it bring you more happiness than my music does me!" He drained his glass all at one swallow and wiped his mouth with the back of his hand. He shuddered like the likker was cold or burnt and Rady noticed his hand was shaking again when he lit a cigarette. He pulled at his mouth. "Cromwell, will you go down there and talk to those people for me? I'll say the wrong thing sure as shooting. I don't know how to talk to the people around here. Make them a fair proposition, and take care of it for me, will you?"

Rady drained his own glass. "Mister Rowe, a man had ort to do his own dealin'. I might not fix it up to suit you."

"Oh, sure you will. You know what's right. Whatever you arrange will suit me fine. Just for God's sake be sure and get me somebody!"

I reckon it was about then that the idea first come to him. The idea of running Mister Rowe's farm himself, with the Pringles to help him out. Mister Rowe was a fool, it was plain to see, and when Rady thought of all those fine acres being wasted he couldn't help feeling like it would be a shame not to use them to his own good advantage. He thought of Annie's little farm, and his thoughts of it were good, for it was a tidy place. But if he could get the Pringles to help he could run both places and there was no knowing what he could make off the two. The particulars never come to him right then, but the idea took hold and commenced growing in his mind. He knew he could do it. And in a way it would be a favor to Mister Rowe. "All right," he said, "I'll do it. I'll go over first thing in the mornin'."

He turned around to go . . . but he stopped. A woman stood in the door. She had come there as quiet as a mouse, and stood there like a statue on a gravestone, still and carved. Her face was white and smooth, like it had been rubbed out of white clay, rounded and slicked, no wrinkles left, no thought or look stamped on it. Just white and smooth. And her hair was as black as the night. It hung all around her face and curled up just a little bit where it touched her shoulders. She just stood there in the door looking at Mister Rowe. It was like Rady wasn't even there. Her arms hung quiet by her side, and she made no motion of any kind except that while she looked at Mister Rowe the pupils of the eyes got bigger. That was all. The rest of her was motionless, like a fall of water caught by ice. Then she came into the room and the stillness of her was broken.

Mister Rowe turned towards her, quick-like. "Oh." He made a move as if to push the whiskey and glasses out of sight, but he caught himself. It was too late. "Cordelia," he said, "this is our neighbor, Rady Cromwell."

She bent her head a little and the black hair swung forward. She spoke to Rady. "How do you do, Mr. Cromwell?" Her voice came out of her throat deeper than most women's, but it had no meaning in it. Just flat . . . even . . . polite.

She looked at him when she spoke, and then she slid her eyes back to Mister Rowe. From him they went to the empty glasses, and they turned hard. Then she laughed. Not a real laugh. Not soft or pretty or careless. Not a laugh that had joy in it at all. A laugh that was as flat and hard as her eyes and her voice, and that never even got past the corners of her mouth, leaving it straight and white and unmoved. It was a laugh like a cold wind blowing, and in its passing Mister Rowe's shoulders quivered and the glass tinkled when he moved his hand against it.

Without saying another word the woman turned and left, the black hair swinging with the speed of her turning, and her shoes on the bare floor made a sharp, crackling sound, like dry limbs being trod in the woods.

Mister Rowe looked at Rady. "Cromwell . . . ?"

As if he'd been told Rady knew. Mister Rowe was sick. Sick inside, and drinking too much to cover it over. The way the woman had acted had said it as plain as day. Mister Rowe stood there and pulled at his twitchy mouth. "Cromwell?"

"I'll see Pringle, Mister Rowe," Rady told him, and he went out through the door himself.

Chapter Six

Rady was as good as his word and the next morning he saddled his mule and rode down to the Pringle place. Old Man Pringle was a beefy, red-faced man, stout as an ox and about as stupid, but he could work twelve and fourteen hours a day without turning a hair. And like Annie'd said, he had a bunch of young'uns to help him. His woman was a toothless old hag, but she was still stout to get around. One eye was crossed, and it used to give me the creeps to be around her, for when she looked at you and talked, it was like she was looking over your shoulder at something standing behind you. They'd always lived either down in the bottoms or over on Bruton's Ridge, so that none of us in our settlement had ever known them too well. Just by hearsay. But a man couldn't be choosey with the season coming up.

Rady rode up to the front gate and hallooed. Old Man Pringle came out, "Howdy," he said.

Rady said the same and talked on a minute or two about the weather, the chances of a good crop this year, the price of cream and eggs and such before he came to the point. A ridge man don't state his business right off. He kind of sidles up to it. But after he'd gone all around Robin Hood's barn, Rady named what he'd come for. "You contracted fer this season?"

Old Man Pringle spit his tobacco juice out and told him no, he'd not made no contract yet.

"Would you keer to make a change?"

"Depends."

"I reckon you've heared they's a new feller on the Hall place up on New Ridge."

"Zat so?"

"Yeah. City feller. Don't know nothin' about farmin'. Made me a proposition to run the place fer him."

Old Man Pringle waited for Rady to go on.

"I'm studyin' on makin' a deal with him, but I'd need some help."

"That's a purty big place, ain't it?"

"Sizable. That's why I'd need some help. I got my own place to tend, too."

"What's yer deal?"

"The usual."

Old Man Pringle studied a while. "Rent from you, or from him?"

"From me."

"Work the Hall place or yore'n?"

"Both."

"Where'd I live?"

"They's a good house on the Hall place. Better'n common."

The old man spit again. "Well, much obleeged to you. I'll study on it."

And Rady rode off, knowing the deal was as good as made.

He let Mister Rowe sweat a day or two, then he went over to have a talk with him. "Pringle ain't very interested in makin' a change, Mister Rowe," he told him.

"You made him a good proposition?"

"Yessir. Jist the usual kind. He don't know about workin' fer a city feller. Figgers he'd lose out in the long run."

Mister Rowe looked white and tired out. Like things were getting the best of him, and he leaned against the gate, drooped and slack. He looked out across those wide fields that to a farming man were the sweetest sight in the world like he wished he'd never seen them before.

"Mebbe you'd ort to of went yerself, Mister Rowe," Rady said, after a time. "I was afeared I'd mess it up fer you."

"No," Mister Rowe said, straightening up. "No. If you couldn't make a deal with him, I'm sure I couldn't have. It's just about what I expected. But I don't know what to do next. I've got to have somebody."

Rady waited a minute more, then kind of gentle-like he made his proposition. He went slow and easy, like he'd just had the notion, kind of letting time slip in between the words. "Mister Rowe, hit jist might be I could help you out myself. Way I git it, you'd ruther have somebody would take over an' kind of run things fer you. Hit might be I could figger out to do it."

Mister Rowe looked at him with a disbelieving look, and then his face come alive with his anxiousness to believe what he was hearing. "You would! My God, Cromwell, that would be the best thing that could possibly happen! I'd not worry a minute if you were in charge!"

"No, sir. That's what I figgered."

"But you've got your own place to farm. How would you manage to run this place and yours too?"

"Well, I'd have to have some help. But I kin pick me up a man by the day I reckon. I'll figger it out. Only thing is, Mister Rowe . . ." and he hesitated like he was might near ashamed to go on.

"Yes."

"Well, not needin' the rent house an' mebbe using' some of my own stuff, a third don't seem quite . . ."

Mister Rowe picked it up fast. "No, of course not. Would half suit you?"

Rady let his breath out soft. That had been the tricky spot. "I kind of hate to take that much. But I'll farm the place good fer you an' make it pay so's you come out with more fer yore half than you would with two-thirds with ary other feller rentin'."

"I believe that! Do we draw up a contract?"

"No, sir. Not less'n you want one. Yore word's good enough fer me."

"And yours is good enough fer me. But let's have a drink on it!"

So they went in the house and had their drink, then Rady

said they'd ought to ride over the place and make some plans. They went out to the barn lot and saddled a couple of horses and rode off. Rady pointed out where old man Hall had had corn the year before. "We'd best grass that this year," he said. And then they looked at the tobacco field. "Needs lime," Rady told him. "Old Man Hall raised good tobaccer, but I figger we kin raise better. We'll not scant none on the manure. That's what makes good tobaccer, an' with the stock you got we'll not need to scant none. An' if I was you I'd quit foolin' with them milk cows. Put 'em to pasture, raise the calves. More money in beef."

Mister Rowe was listening in a way, but in another way he wasn't. "You do it your way, Cromwell. I don't know . . . and the trouble is," he leaned forward in the saddle, his hands folded across the pommel, "the trouble is, I just don't give a damn."

Rady looked at him. He couldn't understand a man feeling like that, but in the back of his mind he knew it was fine for him. It couldn't be better. It would leave him free to run the place his own way. He kind of sucked in his breath.

Mister Rowe pulled at his mouth and laughed. And they turned around and rode back down the fence line.

"Was you raised in the city, Mister Rowe?" Rady asked after a time.

"Yes."

"What kind of work was it you done back there?"

"I was a lawyer . . . of sorts." And then his mouth crimped like he'd chewed down on bitter alum. "The only thing I ever wanted to do in my life was to play the piano. I wanted to be a concert pianist."

"Why didn't you?"

"My father. Wanted me in his office. Long line of Rowe lawyers. He didn't think pianists amount to much. Wouldn't hear of it."

"An' you done what yer pa wanted."

Mister Rowe looked at Rady. "Wasn't much else I could do, was there?"

Rady shrugged. He wouldn't of. In a million years he wouldn't of. But then Rady wasn't Mister Rowe.

Mister Rowe straightened up all at once. "How about going fox hunting tonight?"

"All right by me," Rady said. "You want to kill, or you jist want to take the dogs out fer a run?"

"It doesn't matter. Why?"

"Well, it's pretty hard to kill of a night. Best time's real early of a mornin'."

"Let's run the dogs then. But we can take the guns. Might get a shot."

Rady come got me to go with them, on account of me having three good hounds, and we picked Mister Rowe up right after good dark. I took along a jug for good measure. We all sampled it on the way and Mister Rowe allowed he was going to get plumb fond of moonshine before long.

We went over back of Sawtooth down Croaker Branch and turned the dogs loose. Then we built a fire and set down to wait. The jug passed right frequent and we got to examining one another's guns and telling tall tales. Mister Rowe had a .30 caliber rifle with him that was a beauty and me and Rady handled it and sighted it and would of give our eye teeth for one like it. Rady had an old double-barreled shotgun, twelve gauge, and it even had double hammers on it. Mister Rowe said he hadn't never seen one like it before.

"You'd ort to see his old muzzle-loadin' rifle," I said.

"An old muzzle-loader, huh? I'd sure like to see that one."

So then I told him how Rady come by it, and how he won a turkey shoot with his touch-off.

"You mean you actually made a gun yourself and it would shoot?" he said to Rady, looking like he didn't hardly believe it.

"Hell, that wasn't nothin'," Rady said. "Anybody kin make a touch-off. Nearly all the kids raised around here knows how. Mine was a little fancier, mebbe. Shot a little truer. But I don't reckon they ever was a boy in these hills didn't make hisself a touch-off one time or another."

Mister Rowe swigged on the jug and shook his head. "Country kids sure learn to do a lot of things for themselves, don't they? First gun I ever had was a .22 caliber Harrington-Richards. Dad gave it to me on my fifteenth birthday. But I wasn't allowed to hunt with it unless my tutor was along."

"Yore what?" Rady said.

"The man who taught me. I didn't go to public school."

We'd never heard of such, so there wasn't much we could say. Mister Rowe told us then where all he'd been hunting. New Mexico and Arizona for deer and elk, Wyoming for mountain goats, Alaska for bears. He'd sure been all over. "That," he said, "was before . . . before I was ill."

There was a kind of embarrassed quiet then, like Mister Rowe had pulled a cover from in front of something hid. We didn't know whether to ask how he'd been sick and if he was still sick or what. So we just kept quiet. But the hounds made a distraction just then by giving tongue, and we all sprung up to listen.

"That's yore Queenie," Rady said, "she's found a trail!"

My Queenie has got a high, yipping voice when she's running, and you can't never mistake her. Directly, though, we could hear Drum's big old bass right alongside of her, and the other dogs closing in and laying down. They had it, no doubts about it. Mister Rowe was so excited the firelight glistened off his eyes, and he grabbed his gun. "Not yit," Rady said, "they'll run a while. Jist listen."

They were still way off, so we set down again and passed the jug. But we all had our ears cocked towards the hounds. Never was any music in this world sweet as a pack of hounds running. That's the best part of fox hunting . . . running the dogs. Myself, I don't care nothing about killing. But I'd rather listen to my hounds run than eat fried chicken on Sunday!

We stayed by the fire and listened while the old fox took them up the ridge, down the holler, across the branch and back again. And little by little they came closer. Rady put the jug down and stood up. He looked at me. "The head of the holler, you think?"

"There, or jist back of Simpson's place."

So we lit out. Mister Rowe as anxious as a kid on his first hunt. "You think we can see him in this light?" he asked.

"Dunno," Rady told him. "Hit's pretty dark. But you might git a shot."

We hid in the bushes and waited at the head of the holler, the dogs driving closer every minute. "God, I've got buck fever," Mister Rowe said. "I'm shaking till I couldn't hit the side of a barn!"

Rady laughed. "Don't weary about it. There'll be other foxes if you don't git this un."

And as it turned out we didn't even get the sight of the fox. Just as we thought he was nearing the crossing the dogs circled again and their voices grew fainter. "What happened?" Mister Rowe said.

Both Rady and me were listening and from the sound of the dogs we knew they weren't running now. They were milling and circling. "He's denned," Rady said. "I'm sorry, Mister Rowe."

"You mean it's over?"

"Yessir. With that fox, leastways."

Mister Rowe shifted his gun. "Oh, well. Another time, maybe." He was a good sport about it.

We made our way back to the fire and settled down to do some good solid drinking while we were waiting for the dogs to raise another fox. The moonshine had made us mellow and the fire was making us warm and we were all feeling like kings. Laughing, talking and joking. You know how it is. Specially if you're married. A night to yourself again. A night to be yourself, free and unhampered. Just to be your own man, not the one, for a little while, that sleeps double in a sagging, thin-mattressed bed with a woman, the newest kid whiney and muzzling on the other side of her. Not the one that has to get up at first light the next morning and haul on his overhalls and hitch up his old Beck mule and stumble along behind her down a furrow full of stones and sprout roots. Not the one the kids hang on and call papa. A free man, for a time, a free and new-young and sapling-strong man. With a fire burning bright and you squatted in front of it, and a jug to tilt, the likker hot and good inside you, the dogs yipping off somewheres in the dark, the stars so close the tops of the trees are brushed against them. Man, it's good!

I took a notion to hear Rady sing.

"Naw," he said, put out a little in front of Mister Rowe. "I ain't got my gittar."

"That don't matter." I told him. "You kin sing all right without it."

"Naw."

Mister Rowe got to his feet and swayed a little. "I'll sing." he says, "I'll start us off." And he commenced singing some kind of song in some foreign tongue we couldn't make sense of. Something about a toreador. He had a grand, booming voice to sing with. I'll say that for him, and he sure shouted it out. The sides of the holler fair rung with the echoes. He stood there with his legs spraddled and beat the time with his hand and had himself a fine time. Then he fell over a rock trying to sit down and cussed a blue streak over his barked shin. "Now it's your turn," he told Rady.

So Rady, he sung too. He sung the Turtle Dove, the one I'd always admired. Rady never to say had a voice to brag about, but it was true and he could say the words to a song just like they were a story. In your mind's eye you could see what was happening, just as plain. Sometimes he'd make his voice go down so low it was like a whisper, when the song was sad, that is. And you'd feel like it was your own self grieving so. "'The hills shall fly my little turtle dove,'" he sung, "'before I'm false to the maid that I love.'" Me and Mister Rowe both got to crying.

And the fire died down to red, red coals that hissed like rain falling in the dust. And the likker was heavy inside us, and we thought on all the sadness in the world. Then first thing we knew false dawn was in the sky and I decided I'd better get on home. My eyes were having trouble staying open. "Let's go," I said.

We got to our feet all right, but it took the three of us to prop one another up doing it. Then we took off up the holler and down the road, weaving from one side to the other. "Sing!" said Mister Rowe, and he lined out a song. Me and Rady tried to follow, but the best we could do was burp a little. Then Mister Rowe decided to shoot off all the cartridges in his gun. Just aimed it at the sky and pulled loose! Rady and me followed suit and the night was blasted plumb wide open!

I don't know about Mister Rowe, but Junie wouldn't speak to me for several days over coming home so lit up, and Rady said Annie made him move in the back room for a couple of nights. A woman don't never seem to understand a man's need to bust loose once in a while. Women don't seem to have the need. Or if they do they take it out in scrubbing the floors or washing the quilts or putting new paper on the walls. But anyways they don't like it in a man, and I've never seen one yet didn't get sulky and pouty when a man takes a night off thataway. Reckon it's got something to do with it just being men. It kind of leaves the women-folks out, and I've taken notice a woman don't like her man leaving her out of nothing.

But it was a night we had! A good one. Fox or no fox, and we told ourselves we'd do it again come full moon.

Chapter Seven

Annie didn't like any part of the deal Rady had made with Mister Rowe. Of course she never knew about it for a time, it being men's business and Rady seeing no need to tell her. But she threw a right smart fit when she learned about it.

She all but screeched at him. "Are you losin' yer mind, Rady Cromwell, or have you done an' lost it? That place of his'n is big enough to wear out six men! An' when, pray tell, will you have time to do ary thing to it? What's goin' to happen to yer own place, fer goodness' sakes!"

"I'll tend it. Same as usual. I got it all planned."

Annie switched her skirt loose from a snag that was hung, and she yanked so hard on it she ripped a big hole in her skirt. "Well," she said, jerking at her dress, "that's good news. But it'll take a heap more'n planning to take keer of two places!"

"I kin do it."

Annie moved where he was and laid her hand on his shoulder. "Rady," she said, "I wisht you wouldn't. Hit ain't as if we needed to rent from Mister Rowe. We got aplenty to do. We're makin' out good. What need of more?"

He stood up and put both hands around the curve of her waist, which was some thicker than when he'd first put them there, her adding weight since they were married. "They's allus need for more, Annie," he said. "Jist don't weary yerself. I got it all planned. An' it'll work out fine. Mister Rowe don't know the first thing about farmin'. He's got to have somebody do it right. An' I kin make us twicet as much helpin' him out."

Annie told Junie what she was too proud to tell Rady . . . that it was on account of Miz Rowe she had such objections to him renting from Mister Rowe. She said it was almost more than she could stand . . . the thoughts of Rady seeing Miz Rowe all the time. For he would. She'd always be around some place, and Rady'd be coming and going, and he'd talk to her, and he'd see her white face, and her proud eyes, and her silky, black hair, and her slim, long body. And Annie was short and given to fat, and her hair was streaking gray . . . and she was older . . . old . . .

Annie watched Rady and there was a deep hurt and growing anger inside of her. Why would he want to tend Mister Rowe's place? Why wasn't he satisfied with his own place? What more did he want? Or need? And the hurt came from thinking of Cordelia Rowe, and the anger came from Rady not telling her. She'd heard the stories about Miz Rowe . . . about her white, pretty face and her heavy, coal-black hair. About the way she rode of an evening, and of how she never spoke or passed the time of day with a soul she ever met, but rode past like they were never there. About the way she'd sent that woman servant to the door the few times folks had gone to see her right at first. Sent her with the word that Miz Rowe wasn't at home, when a minute before they'd seen with their own eyes she was. But very few had got up the nerve to go in the first place, and time she'd sent such word to them, nobody cared to venture there again.

It was like I had known it was going to be. She was too handsome a woman not to be a thorn in the flesh to all the womenfolks on the ridge. Just the knowing she was there, hid behind the snow-white curtains that hung at the windows, or riding that big chestnut horse of hers of an evening, just the knowing was troublesome. The knowing rankled every woman on the ridge, Annie amongst them. They talked, when they were together, about her high and mighty ways, about her queerness, about how she must be poorly to be so white and thin. But they thought, when they were alone with their thoughts, about that white, handsome face, that proud-chested body, that thick, heavy hair, and most of them, looking down at their own paunchy stomachs and flat, saggy chest, must of felt hopeless and bedraggled, and must of eaten bitter gall with the looking.

Annie oughtn't to said no more, but her hurt and her anger prodded her on. "Rady," she said, after a time, "I ain't in favor of this trade you've got with Mister Rowe, an' I ain't goin' to stand fer it!"

Rady made no answer.

"You hear me, Rady?" she yelled at him.

"I hear you."

"I'll not have it, I said!"

He moved away from her, slow and careful. "What you aim to do about it?" he said, finally.

"I'll show you what I aim to do about it," she screeched, hoisting up her skirts and flying at him like a cat with a coal of fire tied to its tail. "I'll show you!" and she went flailing at him with both hands, clawing and scratching at his face and neck, drawing blood with every time she dug in.

She took Rady by surprise and he was thrown off balance at first by the weight of her storming up against him, but then he steadied himself, spraddling his legs and planting his feet, and he got a tight grip of her hands and just held onto her. Rady had a grip that could paralyze a grown man and Annie was helpless as a kitten in it, but she kept on kicking and screaming at him a time longer. When she finally give up and quit struggling and was commencing to have some sense again, Rady slapped her . . . and it was no easy lick he give her. It cracked hard against her jaw and he had to turn loose of her to let her fall. When she got up he slapped her down again, on the other side of her face. She just sat there, then, looking up at him kind of dazed and un- understanding. She shook her head, like it was ringing, maybe, inside. Then she buried her face in her hands and commenced crying. Rady stood there and watched her cry a minute. Then he hitched up his belt. "Don't never do that agin, Annie," he said. "Don't *never*, you hear? An' you may as well git used to the idee

I'm goin' to tend Mister Rowe's place. Fer I am. Now git up." And he went out the back door.

Cordelia Rowe had something to say about the deal too. I don't know when Mister Rowe told her Rady was going to tend the place for him, or whether he told her or not. Maybe he didn't. Maybe she just took notice of Rady coming and going about the place and caught on. But anyway, one day a few weeks later when the ground had warmed and dried sufficient for plowing, Rady was putting up the team late in the evening after plowing all day. He'd unhitched and turned the mules loose in the barn lot and was hanging up the harness when she stepped in through the big door.

She was dressed for riding, in those tight pants she wore and a white shirt with a dark jacket over it. Rady figured she'd come to the barn to get her saddle. She'd tied her hair back with a red ribbon and in the gloom of the stable her face, without the black hair around it, looked thin and bare and sharp-boned. She stood there in the barn door, with the light behind her, only her face and the front of her shirt shining white in the gloominess. She had one hand braced across the door and she stood there a minute, not moving, like she was getting used to the dimness in the barn before going inside.

Rady moved and she looked at him, quick and sharp. "You? Cromwell?"

"Yes, ma'am. You want me to catch up yer horse, Miz Rowe?"

"No."

She stepped inside the barn and went over to the wall where her saddle hung on its peg and lifted it down. But she let it slide onto her feet and swung around towards Rady. "Tell that moonshiner friend of yours," she said, the words coming steady but clipped, "that he needn't bring any more of his stuff around here."

Rady walked over and picked up the saddle. "I'll pack this out fer you." he said. "Yes, ma'am. I'll tell him." He went towards the door and blotted out the light. As he passed her he spoke again, and his voice was soft and low. "You think that'll do any good?"

He went on outside and leaned the saddle up against the barn. She stood still inside for a minute, then she followed him out, walking quick and fast after him. "What do you mean?"

"If he don't git it from one feller, he will from another, won't he?"

She raised her hand then and pushed a lock of her hair back from her forehead, and it was a weary motion, like she'd done it so many times before she didn't even know she was doing it. And her wrist was tired in its droop. "I'll take care of that," she said. "You just tell him what I said."

"Yes, ma'am."

"Are you going to help with the place?"

"Yes, ma'am. I'm tendin' it."

"What kind of a contract have you got with Jim?"

"Why, they's not, to say, no kind of a contract, Miz Rowe. We jist worked out a deal. I'm to take keer of ever'thing fer Mister Rowe, on the halves."

She just stood there and looked at Rady. She was slim, not thin the way the womenfolks said, slim as a reed down by the river, and about as whippy, but they were right about her being proud-chested. Even with a jacket over her shirt the curve of her bosom was bold. And the red ribbon on her hair was like a thread of blood wound through the black. A cloud shifted just then and the sun came out like it does sometimes just before it sets, strong and, for a few seconds hard and bright. They both stood there in the light, blinking a little in its brightness, and Rady took notice that where the sun laid across the top of her head the hair was tinged with red. It surprised him, for he would of sworn it was black as a crow's wing. Then the sun went under the bank of clouds again and the light went gray and there was no red at all left in her hair. She spoke. "I suppose," she said, "you'll cheat him out of everything but his eye teeth. He'll be fair game for a smart man, and I take it you're a smart man."

"I think so, ma'am. But I'm not aimin' on cheatin' Mister Rowe."

Rady's overhalls were sweated and dirty, and some of the dust from the fields had settled on his face and grimed it, mixed with sweat and the burn of the sun. He'd taken off his hat and there was a line across his forehead that stood out white where the hatband came. His hair was kinked from not having been combed all day. But he gave no notice if he felt dirty and mucky before her, and he met her look straight and steady.

"Why are you renting from us?"

"Because Mister Rowe asked me to. An' I kin make both him an' me a good profit. That ain't illegal as I've heared of."

She laughed, kind of ugly. "I don't imagine illegality would bother you much."

"No, ma'am. But it won't be necessary." Then he broke her look and turned. "I'll catch up yer horse fer you now, ma'am." He whistled, a shrill, long whistle that brought the horse's head up fast and made him come trotting towards the barn.

"He's never done that for anyone but me," Miz Rowe said.

"He does it fer me now, too," Rady said. He laid the saddle blanket on and smoothed it, then swung the saddle up and cinched it. "He's a fine horse."

"Do you like horses?"

"Well, I've not never had none but work horses, ma'am. But I know a good one when I see it."

Miz Rowe swung up in the saddle and picked up the reins. The horse twitched its head like it knew she was in a hurry. Miz Rowe touched her forehead with her crop, like a man tipping his hat. "Thanks," she said, and she dug her heels into the horse's side. He plunged a time or two, then flashed through the gate and Rady stood and watched them straighten out in a hard run down the road.

The woman could ride all right. And she was a handsome bitch, too. He wondered about a woman like that in bed. Steely and hard. He wondered what she was like melted and softened. Or did she melt and soften? Would a man just wear himself out against the hardness? When a woman as frozen as her thawed, would it be hot and enveloping and drowning . . . a full flood let loose and high tide a man could ride to its ebbing? Or would it be a thin, slack, puny little stream, a trickle that would leave him thirsty and dry? He licked his lips and he found that the saliva in his mouth had dried up and his tongue felt too big and suddenly he wanted a drink . . . a big drink of fiery likker to wet his mouth and slack the cramp in his groin.

He went back in the barn, then, where he kept a jug hid in the hay, taking a nip now and then when he wanted it.

The hay in the barn was dry and warm around him, and the cows made a little noise, lying in the straw in the stalls, stirring, not restless or discontented, but the way a cow with a full stomach and maybe a calf near time to be raised will stir. There was a sharp smell of ammonia from the stalls, sour and prickly, and it mixed with the dry, musty smell of the hay, and Rady stood there a time, smelling it and feeling the content in the barn all around him.

He thought on the next day's plowing and the work laid out for tomorrow. And he thought he'd best be getting the Pringles up on the ridge soon. And he thought on having to get Mister Rowe's tenant house ready for them, and he thought on how he'd break it to Mister Rowe the Pringles were coming and how he was aiming on using the tenant house after all. Break it so's Mister Rowe wouldn't think nothing of it.

And then all his thoughts blurred and ran together, and he could see Miz Rowe standing in the bright band of sunlight, the red showing her hair, and her eyes wide and black as night. Not saying anything. Just standing there. And just thinking on her made him have a cold feeling on the back of his neck and a tight feeling inside him. He thought how she was like a knife, with her white, tight face and slim body, a knife razor-honed, whetted and sharpened to a thin edge . . . a thin, cutting edge. He'd always liked the feel of a tempered blade in his hands, a corn knife, say, or tobacco knife. And he liked the way a corn knife slashed through dried cornstalks, leaving them guillotined and useless in the field. Or the way a honed tobacco knife slid through a tobacco stalk, like a hot knife slicing butter, no grain or jar to it, just smooth and clean and sure. Thinking of Miz Rowe and the way she was edgy and sharp and cold made him have a strung, fiddle-tight feeling inside of him. He wanted to feel the temper of the blade in her. See if she bent or gave. See if she . . . but he gave it over and took another swig from the jug. "The hell with her," he said, stoppering the jug. "The hell with her."

Chapter Eight

When you look back on the way things happen to a man, and the way his life goes, it sometimes seems as if he'd set himself a kind of goal and had headed for it all his life, everything happening with that goal in mind, and all his purposes and aims fixed by it. Like he never lost sight of it for a minute. Like he never thought on any other thing. Like he was besieged and obsessed by it. And with Rady Cromwell it seems more that way than with most.

But when you take it all to pieces and look at it, you can see how he moved little by little, studying only one thing at a time, never fixing even to himself any particular goal in view, but watching sharp and making the most of every chance that come his way. If he was driven by one thing, and one thing only, he never knew it himself. He was just following his own instincts, looking out for himself, and with some pride in his way of knowing what would better him. You might say that always stood out plain in front of him. Bettering himself. Making more for himself. But that seems to be a common enough ambition in most men and nothing peculiar to Rady. On the ridge it meant working more land and working it better. Seeing every way to get the most out of every acre, and turning your hand to get more acres.

Like he told Miz Rowe, Rady never had no intentions of cheating Mister Rowe, and as far as I know he never did. Of course he took an advantage when he made the deal with old man Pringle, unbeknownst to Mister Rowe, to work his own land, but it was not an advantage that would work against him. It was the kind of deal that had to be worked the way Rady worked it. On the quiet. But he knew he could give the Pringles a third of his half share, and still make money for himself. He knew what he could do, and he knew precious few men on the ridge could come close to it. He could get more work out of the Pringles than Mister Rowe ever could, and he could work harder and longer than most, himself. But he didn't want his chances of proving it ruined before he got started. So he slid into it easy and cautious. The time had come, now, when he wanted to move the Pringles to the ridge. It was warming up considerable and corn needed to be in the ground. Pastures needed to be cut soon, and there was a mort of work on both Mister Rowe's place and Rady's needing done all at once.

So Rady took a quart bottle out to his barn and filled it from the jug and slid it into his hip pocket, and then he set out like he'd been doing for a week or more to plow on Mister Rowe's place. Mister Rowe nearly always came out sometime during the day to see how he was getting along, and Rady thought he'd likely have a pretty big thirst on by now, him having done as Miz Rowe said and told Enos Higgins to quit delivering Mister Rowe's jug.

I don't know what time of day Mister Rowe wandered out to take a look at the plowing, but it was mid-afternoon when I happened by and he was setting in the shade of a chestnut oak making mighty good headway on that quart bottle of Rady's then. I'd been fishing. Was plowing that morning when I saw the flying ants swarm out of an old stump and I never even finished the row. Just unhitched my old Beck mule and left the plow where it was at. When the flying ants swarm like that the suckers are on the shoals and a man's losing time to finish a row of plowing. There's always time to plow, but when the suckers are shoaling, there's no time to lose. I caught me a string as long as my arm, too, running all the way from ten to eighteen inches.

When I came alongside the field where Rady was plowing I yelled at him and held the string of fish up where he could see.

He pulled his team around in the shade and came over to take a closer look. "Doggone," he says, "them's pretty. Where'd you catch 'em?"

"This side the Beaver Hole," I says. "Could of got twicet as many. Jist got wore out haulin' 'em in."

"Man," he says, "they shore make my mouth water!" Then he grinned. "Reckon these'll cool Junie's temper off some."

"That's what I'm hopin'," I says, grinning back at him. Junie's a mighty fine woman, and I'd not allow nobody to say otherwise, but it's a fact she's quick-spoke, and being a hard worker herself she's got little patience with them that ain't. Liking to fish and hunt like I do, there's been times when she's been right put out at me. Rady's about the only man could josh with me about it, though, and get by with it. But Rady'd known Junie longer than I had, and wouldn't of been any use me trying to hide her notionness from him. Facts is, I'd kind of looked askance at that first young'un of ours more'n once, him being born a couple of months too soon the way he was, and me knowing it wasn't on my account he come too soon. But after I knew Junie better I figured he was a seven-months young'un like she said, for if she was as hard to corner *after* it was legal and proper, I allowed not even Rady Cromwell could of got to her without. "I figger," I says to him, "these'll kind of offset me not gittin' that cornfield done today."

"They might," he allowed. "I been thinkin' some of goin' fishin' myself come Sunday."

"Suckers'll all be gone by then," I told him. "You better take off an' go this evenin'."

He shook his head. "Got too much to do."

Mister Rowe pulled himself to his feet then and walked over, kind of hanging onto the fence to steady himself. He was a handsome man, all right, there's no denying. But there's something about seeing a man drink himself into limberness of a daytime that's never set good with me. I've been drunk my share of times, but it's always been done decent-like, of a night when I was coon hunting or fox hunting, or out roistering around with the boys. I don't hold with daylight drinking. Mister Rowe was mighty unsteady on his feet, but he pulled himself along the fence to where we were standing. "He's got too much to do," he said, solemn as an owl, his head wobbling on his neck and his eyes kind of glazed. "Rady's a very busy man. Got too much to do to go fishing. But I can go fishing. I've not got too much to do. Rady's taking care of everything and I can go with you. Just say when."

"Well, not right now, Mister Rowe." I says, "I just been. I got to go on home now and do up the work."

"Just say when," he droned on, "just say when. Now or then, it doesn't make any difference. I can go. Rady's got too much to do, but I can go."

"You better go set down, Mister Rowe," Rady said. "Go on back an' set down in the shade. You don't want to git a sunstroke now with all that likker inside you."

Mister Rowe looked at Rady like a kid looking at a grown-up, trusting and kind of puzzled-like. Then he put his hands up over his head like he was keeping the sun off and turned around and commenced backtracking. "No. I don't want to get a sunstroke, do I? Not with all this liquor inside me. When I go fishing I can get the sunstroke too, can't I?" And he leaned up against the tree and slid down its trunk.

Rady laughed. "He shore was dry."

"How much has he had?"

"Best part of that quart. He had the shakes all right."

"Liable to kill him!"

Rady shook his head. "Naw. He'll sleep it off."

I looked out across the field Rady was plowing. Like everything else he did, Rady did a nice job plowing. "How you gittin' along?" I asked.

"Fine," he says, "jist fine. Fixed it with Mister Rowe today to let the Pringles have his tenant house, an' I'll be gittin' them up here soon now. Git that old man an' them boys to workin' an' ever'thing'll move faster."

He was grinning and I knew then how come Mister Rowe to be limber. I couldn't help laughing. "Looks like you fixed Mister Rowe."

"Jist a mite," he says. "Figgered it wouldn't hurt none. Make it kind of painless fer him."

He held his hand up to measure the sun. "Jist a coupla hours left. I got to git back to my plowin'."

I hefted my string of fish and pulled out and Rady swung his team around out of the shade.

He finished up the day's stint and left Mister Rowe with his bottle in the shade until he'd put up the team, then he went back to take him to the house. "Got any left?" he asked.

Mister Rowe just blinked at him, not hearing what he'd said nor able to take in its meaning had he heard. "Come on," Rady told him, "let's go home."

He pulled him to his feet and commenced walking him along the edge of the field, but Mister Rowe was too far gone to walk, so Rady hoisted him like a sack of meal over his shoulders and took him in. At the back door he let him slide down in a heap at his feet, and knocked on the door. Miz Rowe came. She looked at her husband and then she looked at Rady. "He come by a bottle, ma'am. I've brung him home."

"I see," she said. "Where did he get it?"

Rady shrugged his shoulders. "A man allus knows ways, Miz Rowe. Hit does little good to forbid him."

"I haven't forbidden his drinking, Cromwell," she said. "The doctors have forbidden it. He isn't allowed any alcohol at all. If he doesn't stop drinking, it will kill him."

She wasn't dressed in her riding clothes that day, and she stood in the door in a blue dress that tied around the middle with some kind of a sash that made her look more like a girl than a woman, banding her waist so that it looked small enough a man's two hands could span it. And there was pink in her checks from the heat of the stove where she'd been cooking supper. Rady could see past her into the kitchen that was like no other kitchen on the ridge, with its brightness and color and shining cleanness. Everything about the house was like Miz Rowe herself, clean, shiny, in place, and the curtains that hung in the kitchen were as snow white as those in the rest of the house.

Rady looked down at Mister Rowe, limp at his feet, and Miz Rowe looked too. "Bring him in," she said then.

Rady slung him over his shoulder again and followed her

through the house into the bedroom. It was the downstairs bedroom and she motioned for Rady to put Mister Rowe on a tall,
four-poster bed with a canopy of some thin white stuff spread
over it. When Rady'd put him down he looked around, and he
knew he'd never in all his life seen so pretty a bedroom. So quiet.
So clean. So kept. Shiny floors, shiny furniture, white spreads
and walls. Clean and uncluttered and uncrowded. He took a deep
breath, for I reckon he was seeing it against what he'd been used
to all his life, a straw tick on a loft room floor when he was a boy,
and now an iron bedstead with a patchwork quilt of Annie's making for a coverlid.

We're lucky on the ridge if we've got as much as a spare
room to put a bedstead in. Mostly we've got to crowd beds into
every room on the place excepting the kitchen, and mostly we
don't worry nor care. I reckon beauty inside a house is something
we don't know much about. The women-folks take a pride in their
flower pretties in the yards, and the smartest of them are not
content unless things are tolerably clean, but there's few places
not cluttered with a sizable brood of young'uns, and there's no
woman on earth can keep a house redd up good with eight or
nine kids and a man to do for, in two or three rooms.

Annie had got Rady used to something better than he'd ever
had before, but Annie was a ridge woman too, and paper roses in
a fruit jar on the mantel and bright pink curtains from the mail
order were awful pretty to her. Rady'd not seen prettiness made
out of space and order and whiteness and shine. But he knew the
Rowes well enough by now to know that whatever they had; and
whatever they did, had come from the ways of money and good
living. The room looked empty to him, but he liked it, and he
knew if the Rowes had it, it was right.

"I can manage now, thank you," Miz Rowe said, and she stood
aside for Rady to leave.

"I'd be glad to undress him fer you." Rady said. "Fer all he's
thin he's right hefty fer a woman."

She smiled at him, but it wasn't much of a smile, just a
shadow and gone as soon as it was glimpsed. "Do you think I
haven't had a lot of practice?"

"I wouldn't know."

"Well, I have. And I can manage perfectly well, thank you." She bent over and commenced unlacing Mister Rowe's shoes. Then she straightened. "By the way, don't mention what I've told you. He doesn't like for people to know."

"No, ma'am."

And she went back to tugging at Mister Rowe's shoes.

The next day Rady got Annie to go with him to clean up the tenant house. Not that it would of made much difference to the Pringles, for they were counted as slovenly and dirty in a house as folks could be and no matter how clean a place was when they moved in, it didn't take them long to make a shambles of it. Nor did Annie much care about going over and helping clean for them. "Why?" she asked Rady. "They'll jist have it like a pigsty in a month's time. Jist let 'em move in the way it is."

"That ain't my way of doin'," Rady said. "Git you some soap an' rags an' come on."

She muttered around a time but she got her a kettle of soft soap and bundle of rags and made ready to go. "I dislike goin' over to the Rowes'," she said finally. "Supposin' Miz Rowe come around!"

"Supposin' she does? She ain't no witch nor nothin'."

"No, I reckon not!" Annie snapped at him. "Fur from it, facts is. But I got my pride, Rady Cromwell, an' I ain't keerin' to have Miz Rowe seein' me wash down a tenant house!"

"Hit's got to be done," Rady said. "An' what's pride got to do with it?"

"A heap," she mumbled, but grumbling or no she went with him.

It wasn't in too bad shape and they cleaned it out and scrubbed it down and Rady said he'd come back the next day and whitewash. "When they aimin' on movin' in?" Annie asked.

"Soon as we git the house ready. Next day or two."

"I've heared that the oldest girl is hired out over in town." Annie said. "That'll be one less hand you'll have."

"I ain't wearied none," Rady said, "about the girls. It's the old man an' the boys I'm countin' on. Never did hold with girls workin' in the fields. Never seen one yit could hold out good."

"Well, they say Flary kin. I've heared it said she was as good as ary boy ever taken hold of a hoe. An' she kin plow, too. Of course she ain't, to say, real bright, but she kin work."

"They's enough with the old man an' the boys."

When they finished inside the house they raked over the yard and picked it up and Rady stoutened a paling or two in the fence. It was getting along towards midday when they quit. "I'd ort," Rady said, "to go by an' see how Mister Rowe's feelin', I reckon. He wasn't very peart yesterday."

"Don't count none on me goin' with you! I'm headin' fer home."

"Go ahead. I'll be there time you git dinner ready."

Miz Rowe was eating her dinner out in the side yard under a big mulberry tree grew there. She did things different like that, and she had a little table spread with a white cloth and a bouquet of crocus from down the side of the brook in the middle. She looked up when Rady came around the corner of the house. "Hello," she said, and she waved her hand at one of those deck chairs stood on the walk close by. "Sit down."

"I got to be gittin' on. Jist come by to see how Mister Rowe was."

"Still in bed. But conscious and moaning. He's got a terrific headache."

Rady grinned. "I kin well imagine."

She was friendlier than she'd been before and Rady thought it was likely on account of him knowing now about Mister Rowe. It was like she'd kind of eased up on her guard a little. "Will you have some lunch?" she asked, but she made no move to get up. Like she knew he wouldn't, which he wouldn't of. Not for nothing in this world.

"No'm. I'll eat when I get home."

"What have you been doing this morning?"

"Cleanin' up the rent house. I'm havin' a family move in this week. Mister Rowe said it was jist settin' there empty an' if I needed it to make free with it."

She was eating some kind of soup and she laid her spoon

down dainty on the plate alongside the bowl and wiped her mouth. "I thought you didn't intend to cheat."

"I'm not. I'll pay the Pringles out of my half."

"How will you make anything for yourself that way?"

Rady pushed his old hat on the back of his head and laughed. "Well, you're right, Miz Rowe, a third never was as much as a half."

She laughed, too, then. "According to my arithmetic it's not either." She pushed her chair back from the table and stood up. "Do you need anything for the house? There's a lot of stuff around here still packed away."

"No, ma'am. Hit ain't necessary to furnish a house with no house plunder. Jist the house an' use of the garden patch an' barns an' sich. They'll make out fine."

With her standing like that he felt like he had when he was a boy in school and the teacher had said class dismissed, so he told her good-day and pulled out.

He felt pretty good about everything. Getting the Pringles up on the ridge and the way things were going. And it made him feel fine that Miz Rowe was thawing out a little. He allowed if she came to trust him as well as Mister Rowe he could come closer to running things to suit himself. Not that he wouldn't of found ways to do that anyhow, but it made it easier to have both of them depending on him and abiding by his word. He figured Mister Rowe wouldn't never argue the question with him, but Miz Rowe could easy be a right rough handful should she get her head set against him like it looked like she was going to at first.

The Pringles moved their house plunder, their cows and their pigs and theirselves the last of the week, and it was a sight to see. They got the house plunder in one old wagon, and set the kids around any old place on top the load. They tied the cow to the back of the wagon, and the old man drove the pigs in front, the oldest boys helping him. Miz Pringle set in the wagon seat and drove the team. About as sorry a looking outfit as was ever seen going down the road.

Rady put the old man and the boys to work first thing the next morning planting corn, and after he saw to it they were started good and had their understanding of the work laid out for them the next day or two, he went on home and commenced planting on his own place. He was aiming on putting out a right smart of corn that year, on account of going to buy some more calves that fall to run on both places. Regardless of how good a pasture you got, it does take corn to fatten beef, and he wasn't intending to run short through the winter.

Time went past the slow way it does when the days get hot and the skies get blue and faraway looking. There's no prettier time in this world than May on New Ridge, when the timber takes on its dressing and the flowering bushes and trees bust out. I love the honey locusts best. In May the limbs hang heavy with sweet-smelling blooms and the bees swarm amongst the flowers and get drunk on the sweetness, and a man can stand under the limbs and have every sound in the air drowned out by the steady humming all around him. He can stand there until his head swims with the sound and nothing is real but the strong humming. And when he comes away, if he looks he'll see his hat brim is snowed with the little waxy petal of the blooms that have fallen while he stood.

May is the time for planting, too, and the ground is loose and ready for the seed, and the color is brown with gray and black mixed in. Little new tobacco plants are the lightest green you ever saw, and they're fuzzy and proud-looking and tender. They look so little when you put them in the ground, and it's hard to believe they'll ever be as tall as a man's head with leaves as broad as a foot ruler can measure. It's hard to believe, too, the work they'll take, but when a season comes in May and you commence setting tobacco, it's like you'd never done it before. You set with a gladness to be handling the earth and the growing green plants, not minding the hot summer ahead and the long days of hoeing and plowing and tending. Just with a springing up of something fine inside and a kind of singing that you've got a piece of land and something to tend.

May is the best month for fishing too, and when Junie and me and the kids had the tobacco set I nearly fell over one day when she said she'd go along to the creek with me and wet a hook herself. When we were courting she'd gone with me some, and she was a good hand to catch sun-fish and red-eye. But it had been such a time since she'd had a hankering to go that I was real surprised at her. She fixed up a basket of stuff to eat against we might have good luck and stay out after dark, and the kids scampered around like a bunch of coon hounds let loose, so glad to be going.

They scattered when we got to the creek and me and Junie set our poles alongside of one another in the shade. For a time we caught a few, and then the fish got lazy like they do in the middle of the afternoon, and I laid back down on the ground and dozed off. But not for long. Junie had something on her mind to say and she waked me up after a little. "Did you know that Annie is goin' to the doctor over in town?" she said.

I rubbed my eyes with my fists, not knowing why it mattered if she was. "Is she?" I said.

"She is. I thought mebbe Rady'd said something to you."

"No."

"Likely she ain't told him. I wouldn't of thought she would."

"What's she goin fer?"

"Well, it don't make sense to me. She told me in confidence, but I reckon a woman's man keeps the confidence. She says to me one day last week, she says, 'I'm aimin' on tryin' to have me a baby, Junie, an' the doctor, he's helpin' me.' I says to her, 'Ain't that goin' agin' nature, Annie? I'd be askeered of sich.' She says, 'I ain't askeered of but one thing. I'm askeered he might not fix me so's I kin.'"

When Junie commences telling something there's nothing to do but get comfortable and listen, so I laid easy and folded my arms under my head and tipped my hat over my eyes. She peered under the hat brim. "Are you listenin'?"

"I'm listenin'. Annie said she wasn't askeered of nothin' but mebbe the doctor couldn't fix her up."

"Well, it beats all! I says, 'Annie,' I says, 'why are you so set on havin' a young'un all of a sudden?' I says, 'Hit'll likely be awful resky.' But she jist shook her head an' says she'll take the resk. I says, 'The Lord would of sent you a young'un before now,

Annie, if He was minded fer you to raise one. Hit appears to me to be goin' agin His will.' She says, 'I allow He won't be keerin' if me'n the doctor helps Him out a mite.' I says, 'Well, as for me, I'd a sight ruther not commence nothin' like that. You got things easy, Annie Cromwell, an' hit looks like you'd want to leave 'em thataway.' Now what do you think of that?"

"I think that it's hers an' Rady's business, that's what I think of it," I say, setting up. "You told her what you had a mind to, an' now jist keep yer nose out of it. Don't go talkin' it up an' down the ridge."

She got so mad the sparks flew. "Well, fer heaven's sake! I've not said ary word to a soul but you, an' I've knowed fer a week or more! I reckon I kin keep a confidence when I'm a mind to!"

"Jist see that yer a mind to, then. Tellin' me was all right, but don't tell nobody else."

She just sniffed and stuck her nose up in the air. But I got a bite then and I paid her no heed.

She watched me land the fish and bait my hook again and then she said, "Of course I never come out an' said my whole mind about it. I never said hit was about the boldest thing I'd ever heared tell of!"

I strung the fish. "What's bold about it?"

"Why, her goin' to a man doctor over in town an' talkin' to him so, an' Lord knows what lettin' him take the advantage of!"

I was plumb disgusted. Of course Junie had Granny Williams with all of ours, but yet had she wanted a doctor I wouldn't of had no objections. "Christ's sake, Junie,' I said, "the man's a doctor. I reckon he's used to women gittin' ready to drop a young'un."

"Mebbe so," she said, "but he wouldn't git no usedter to it with me!"

"If they's ever ary thing wrong with you, Junie," I says, "that you need to see the doctor, I'm takin' you to him, an' you might as well make up yer mind to it!"

"Hit had not better be no higher than my knee, then," she says, "fer I ain't h'istin' my skirt fer no man, doctor or not!"

I couldn't help but laugh. But I will say it's a right smart comfort to a man, knowing his woman is like that. Ain't much chance him being made a fool of behind his back. But all I said was, "Jist mind what I told you an' keep outen it."

Going by what Rady's said to me that time about it's being a God's blessing not having young'uns, I wondered what he was going to think about this. It didn't go queer to me that Annie would be wanting a kid. It sounded right natural to me. I just hoped the best for her and kind of snickered at the idea of Rady being a papa. Boy, was I ever going to have fun with him! The bigger they are, the harder they fall, I thought, and I knew why the menfolks would take Rady for a high old time when that young'un come! I kind of wished for him a boy, but about that time my oldest fell in the creek and like to of drowned before I could haul him out. Then when I slung him onto the bank he landed on a fishhook and it cost me two dollars to have the doctor cut it out of his bottom! I figured then a girl would be better for Rady after all. Not having none, all mine being boys, I couldn't say for sure, but they couldn't be as much trouble to raise as boys. I wouldn't reckon they'd go around falling into creeks and setting on fishhooks, leastways.

That was the last time Junie ever went fishing with me. She allowed if I couldn't keep an eye on my own kids and keep them from harm's way, it wasn't safe for her or them to go along. Which suited me just as well. Women and kids don't mix with fishing.

Chapter Nine

We had a hot summer that year. Hot and muggy, with a lot of rain. It rains considerable in our parts any season, but it kind of outdid itself that summer, coming a hard downpour might nigh every week. When it rains that often, a man's hard-put to keep his work up, for the ground'll be too soft to hoe or plow for a couple of days afterwards, and by the time he can give it a going-over, it comes another rain and he's not got anywhere. The heat and the wet makes crab grass and careless weed grow rank and before you can say scat, it's just about taken your crop. Wasn't a man of us didn't have his hands full the whole season.

I saw Rady in passing several times and he admitted it was taking the full time of him and the Pringles to keep ahead on both places and was times when it looked like it was more than they could do. But I misdoubt the old Scratch himself could of kept Rady from tending those crops, he was so bent on making good that year. And what he had out looked a heap better than most. Leastways the weeds never got so far ahead of him that him and the Pringles had to get down on their knees and uproot them by hand like I did! But they got started sooner of a morning than most, and I've met Rady going home of an evening when the moon was making light.

It must of been along in July Mister Rowe took a notion he

wanted Rady to learn him how to play the gittar and sing some of
the song-ballats he knew so many of. When Rady was putting
the team up one Saturday night, a little earlier than common on
account of it being meeting night and Annie wanting to go, Mister Rowe came out to the barn. "Cromwell," he said, "how about
coming over a little while tonight and bringing your guitar and
giving me a lesson? I've got a new book of arrangements of some
of those old ballads and it would be fun to go over them."

He'd fleshened up some, eight or ten pounds maybe, and
while he still pulled at his mouth and gave other signs he was
fidgety and twitchy, he looked better than he had when they moved
to the ridge, and of late folks passing would hear the piano playing and figured it was him playing. At first he hadn't ever touched
the piano. Myself, I thought it was a pity his pa hadn't let him
take up piano-playing, for in my opinion he was powerful good at
it. Not that I was an expert on judging, but he could really romp
all over it, there wasn't no two ways about it.

Rady was undecided what to do, for he'd given his word to
Annie to go to meeting with her and he knew she'd be madder
than a hornet did he back out on it. But he sure did like to play
his gittar and sing, and it had been a time and a time since he'd
done much of it. "I don't know, Mister Rowe," he said after pondering it a minute. "I kind of promised Annie I'd go to meetin'
with her tonight."

"Meeting? Oh," Mister Rowe said, "church. Do they have
church here on Saturday night?"

"Yessir. We have it of a Saturday night, instead of a Sunday,
bein's they's no regular preacher now. Hit's more of a prayer
meetin' than church. But the folks git together ever' Saturday
night."

"Oh, well. Let it go. It was just an idea. I thought you might
enjoy it too."

"I would," Rady said. "Would tomorrer do? Hit bein' Sunday
I could come then all right."

Mister Rowe looked sluggish and like it didn't much matter.
"I guess so. I needed a drink right away though," and he looked
at Rady and grinned kind of sheepish.

"What's the matter? Yer bootlegger gone back on you?"

"Yes, dammit! He hasn't been around in a couple of months. I haven't had a drop except what you've brought me a time or two. When you see him, tell him I need a jug."

Rady shook his head. "They've been layin' off of late, Mister Rowe. Been skeered up a little. New sheriff an' the boys ain't takin' no chances. I misdoubt I kin git Enos to bring you any."

"Well, have you got any?"

"Jist a little. Not more'n a pint. But you're welcome to it. An' I kin fix you up tonight. I'll leave it at the gate as we go past yore place on the way to meetin'."

Mister Rowe heaved a sigh. "That'll be fine."

Rady didn't know whether Mister Rowe knew Miz Rowe had told him he wasn't supposed to have any. He kind of doubted Miz Rowe telling him she'd told. But he didn't see how a little, just a couple of drinks now and then, could hurt anybody. So he'd passed a pint to Mister Rowe once or twice when it looked like he needed it real bad. "That'll be fine," Mister Rowe said, and then he laughed. "How'll you keep Annie from seein' you?"

Rady laughed too. "Well, a guy kin allus stop to take a leak, can't he?"

"What if she stops to wait for you?"

"She won't. I'm real modest about takin' a leak."

Leaving that pint at the gate was why Mister Rowe never felt like singing song-ballats the next afternoon. Not that he couldn't of got over a pint by the next afternoon, but it made him sick, drinking it all down so quick that night, and he couldn't lift his head off the pillow the next day without heaving.

When Rady came with his gittar Miz Rowe opened the door to him. She must not of known Rady was coming for she looked kind of surprised when she saw him, especially with his gittar strung around his neck. "Are you going to serenade someone?" she said, motioning to the gittar.

Rady ran his thumb across the strings and the gittar whanged. "Me an' Mister Rowe was aimin' to practice up on some song-ballats this evenin'. He said come over."

"He's sick."

"Why, he was feelin' real peart yesterday evenin'! Was it somethin' he eat?"

She stepped back in the hall and swung the door wide. "Oh, come on in. No, it wasn't something he ate. He got hold of some whiskey again."

Rady was real busy with the cord on his gittar, getting it over his head. "Well, I declare," he said, "that's too bad."

Rady was used to having to keep womenfolks in the dark and it went easy for him. But he never liked it that the whiskey had made Mister Rowe sick. It looked like Miz Rowe was right and he hadn't ought to drink a drop. It was kind of a bad place to be in, with Mister Rowe nagging for it all the time.

Miz Rowe led him into the room where the piano was. "Now that you're here," she said, "you might as well play and sing for me."

Rady felt shy about playing for her. It was different with a man, or the ridge folks. But just to cut loose and sing in front of Miz Rowe scared him a little. "Hit might bother Mister Rowe," he said.

"No, it won't. He's asleep right now. Go ahead. Where do you want to sit?"

"Anywheres'll do. Jist so it's a straight cheer."

When he'd set down he fiddled with the gittar strings, putting off getting started, but Miz Rowe set down across the room from him and folded her hands in her lap like she was ready to listen, so he figured he had to plunge into it. "I'm not very good," he said, "an' hit's a time sincet I picked a gittar, so likely I'll make a lot of mistakes."

Of course Miz Rowe never knew it was manners to discount yourself no matter how good you were. Rady knew he was better than most on the gittar. Miz Rowe just said, "I'll never know the difference. Go on."

"Well, all right," and he swallowed his Adam's apple and commenced. He sung her about half a dozen . . . "Down in the Valley," "Barby Allen," "The Tree in the Wood" and some more, and he wound up with "On Top of Old Smokey." All as pretty songs as you ever heard.

Miz Rowe listened polite enough, but when Rady kind of run down she never thanked him nor said the songs were pretty nor she'd liked them or anything. She just set a minute and then she laughed, kind of short. "Music hath charms . . ." she said. And then she swung her hair back from her face and laughed again. "That was quite a concert, Cromwell. Very educational. The original and doubtless the most admirable of the old folk songs. But what the hell," and she turned towards him and spit the words out as fierce and pointed as darts, "what the hell is admirable about folk songs? Just why is 'On Top of Old Smokey' worth saving? I find it dreary!"

Rady felt like a fool for having opened his mouth, and he wished he'd had sense enough to turn on his heel when he found out Mister Rowe was sick. That was what come of showing off, he thought, for he knew that was what he'd been doing. And it made him mad at himself for having done it. And mad at her for having showed him up. So mad that the bile spewed up in his throat and mouth, and his hands shook as he laid the gittar down. The bitch, he thought. The gahdamned, cold-blooded, mean-tempered, frost-bitten bitch! And because his hands were shaking so, and because she was still standing there looking at him, he put them deep in his pockets for fear the only way he could steady them would be around that white neck of hers, where he could squeeze tight and choke off her scorn and laugh and the spiked, needling words. He held onto himself hard and looked at her straight.

He couldn't help but look at her neck, and then, thinking how it would feel to squeeze his fingers around her neck, it come over him how soft it would be. How smooth her skin was, and how white. And how his hands would lie against it, hard and callused, feeling the softness in his palms. And how his hands would move, then, to the rest of her softness and whiteness . . . over and cupping the fine, bold breasts, around and under into the soft, cushiony armpits where the flesh was tender as a baby's. Down and around the curving waist and on, until, finding, a man's hands could finally rest. He wanted to lay her then and there. Strip her and have her and get rid of his own swollen wanting. And he hated her because he couldn't have her. He hated her so strong he didn't dare to open his mouth or he'd have said things would of made enemies of them forever. He wanted to spill out all the ugly, mucky words he knew and dirty her with them and humble her.

But he didn't. He kept his mouth shut, and it was Miz Rowe who spoke first. "That was beastly of me, Cromwell. I'm in a foul mood today. I always am when Jim gets hold of whiskey. But, oh God, why must men be such fools!"

Except for his hands still shaking Rady had got hold of himself now and his voice came steady enough when he answered her. "I've never noticed they was any bigger fools than wimmen, Miz Rowe. Hit seems to be human nature in general fer a body to make a fool of hisself once in a while. Jist as I've done today. I'd ort to of knowed you'd think the song-ballats was foolish an' tiresome."

She made an impatient move with her hands. "Oh, no. Your songs were just something to catch at. Just one more thing. One more man who likes music! I've said I'm sorry. Now let's forget it."

It never took very deep studying to figure that Mister Rowe's piano-playing was what she thought made a heap of his trouble. And likely it did. If a man's heart is set on a thing and it's denied him and he can't put it out of his mind, it's likely to rankle pretty deep. Rankle till, like it was doing to Mister Rowe, it makes him sick and sour inside. It was plain and clear to Rady that Miz Rowe didn't much like music, and he vowed she'd never hear another note out of him. "I'd best be goin'," he said.

"No, I want to talk to you," she said. "Come on out to the kitchen and I'll make some sandwiches. I'm hungry and we can talk as we eat."

He followed her to the kitchen and she made a plate full of sandwiches and a pitcher of lemonade and they set at the kitchen table and eat. It was nice in the kitchen. The heat was going out of the day and the kitchen was on the shady side of the house and felt cool and big. It was low-ceilinged, like all our ridge houses, and she'd had the sheathing taken off the ceiling so's the old house beams showed, and she'd painted them white. She had lots of ideas like that, different from ours, and the funny thing was, queer as they went at the time, they always turned out all right. Like those beams now. Wouldn't none of us of thought of having them showing that way. We'd of considered it rough and unfinished. But she'd got her way in spite of what the men did the work said, and now they looked nice . . . cool and low and white, with an old oil lamp hanging over by the table, and strings of red peppers and garlic and onions over by the wall. She thought they were pretty too.

They set and eat, Rady feeling kind of uneasy eating like that with her, and he never to say liked sandwiches. They had some kind of cheese and soft stuff mixed up in them, and like most men he always thought sandwiches had too much bread and not enough filling. But he figured she had something on her mind and he'd best give her a chance to get it told. So he swallowed them down and drunk the lemonade, and waited till she was ready to talk. Which was soon enough. "Are we going to make anything this year, Cromwell?" she asked when they'd both eat.

"Why, yes, ma'am. Ort to do right good."

"This rain hasn't affected the crops?"

"Well, hit's kept us humpin', but we've stayed ahead, an' the crops is in right good shape."

"You're not worried about them, then?"

"I ain't the least bit wearied, Miz Rowe. I don't do much wearyin', you might say. Usual, if they's ary thing to weary about, I git busy an' do somethin' about it."

She heaved a sigh. "That's good. I've been worrying. We need a good crop this year."

"Yes, ma'am. Mister Rowe told me."

She looked at him sharply. "Did he?"

"Yes, ma'am. He said you all had put might nigh ever'thing you had into buyin' this place, an' you'd have to make money on it to live."

"Well, that's near enough the truth. His father won't do anything more for him."

"This is kind of his last chance then?"

"You might say that . . . yes." And she stood up and commenced cleaning the dishes off the table. Having said what she had to say it was like she was dismissing him again, and Rady got up too.

"Well, they's nothin' to weary about this year, anyways. An' I've got plans to do better next season." He said it as innocent as a new-born babe, but he wanted her to know how the land lay.

And she caught on. "You're planning on handling the place next season, then?"

"Unless Mister Rowe wants to git somebody else." Rady knew now he had them where he wanted them. He had them worried, helpless and depending on him.

Miz Rowe was too smart not to see some of that herself. She stacked the dishes in the sink and laughed. "That's not very likely."

"No'm. I never thought so."

He watched to see if that shot went home. That there wasn't anybody else. Just him. He watched her bent over the dishes, and when her shoulders kind of quivered like a little scared rabbit's, he knew she had understood. "I'll go now," he said, and he went and got his gittar. Then he set off for home.

He didn't feel like quite so much of a fool, now. He had found the way to get back his own feeling of pride and power. He was the one on top. They had to have him. He knew it, and now Miz Rowe knew it, and that was good.

Chapter Ten

The way Rady passed, coming and going to the Rowes' place was through the patch of woods laid between his place and theirs. It was as pretty a woodsy place as there is on the ridge. Laid on a gentle slope, with hardly no undergrowth, and the trees were tall, old beech, chestnut, oak and ash which hadn't been cut over in a hundred years. That had given them time to grow thick and heavy, so that the woods were a shady, gladey place, always cool on the hottest day. Down at the foot of the slope ran a narrow little branch, spring-fed so that it never ran dry, and it added some to the coolness of the woods. Lady's-slippers grew rank on its banks, and wild ferns and water hyacinths. Up on the slope there was a fair stand of ginseng and goldenseal. And May-apple grew there in right smart quantity too. It was real sightly and always a pleasure to pass through.

Rady was following the path home that Sunday, when he heard a sound off to the left, down by the branch. He looked, quick, and there was a girl setting on a flat rock by the side of the branch, dangling her feet in the water. It was her had loosened some stones that fell in the water and had made the noise.

Flary Pringle was about sixteen then. She looked older, though, being as big and well-grown as she was. She was a stout, strong girl, big all over. Big-shouldered, big-busted, big-hipped and big-bottomed. Wasn't a thing scrawny or pin-plucked about Flary. Her clothes always looked like they were about to bust their seams on account of being stretched so tight over her body. She was a good-looking girl without being what you'd call pretty. She was dark-complected like the old man, but she had a smooth skin, stretched tight across the bones of her face, and when she was clean she made a real handsome appearance. But she wasn't given to washing too often and there was nearly always a kind of sour smell about her. Some said she wasn't real bright, and it may be she wasn't. She hadn't gone to school but to the third grade, and they said she had trouble learning that far. But she didn't look stupid. Just always had a kind of easy, good-natured look on her face.

Rady stood and looked at her and she stared back at him. She had big, round eyes, brown and soft and melty-looking, like a cow's. "Who are you?" Rady said after a time, walking a little way towards her. I reckon he'd not ever seen her before.

"Flary," she said, and she ducked her head like a kid that's put out with being taken notice of.

"Oh," Rady said, going on down to the branch. "You're Flary Pringle. I thought you was hirin' out over in town."

"I am. I jist come home fer Sunday." She tried to draw her feet up under her skirt, but the skirt was too skimpy. She was setting on the opposite side of the branch, but it wasn't more than two foot wide so Rady just stepped across.

He grinned at her and looked at her strong, brown legs. "Don't mind me," he said, "go ahead an' dangle 'em. Believe I'll cool my feet too."

He sat down beside her and took off his shoes and socks and stuck his feet in the water. "Feels good," he said. "What you been doin' here in the woods? Soakin' yer feet all afternoon?"

She pulled her skirt down as far as it would go and cut her eyes around at him. But she didn't say anything.

Rady reached down and splashed water on his feet, and then like it was an accident he splashed it higher so's it got her skirt wet. He splashed it good and high, too. She stood up real quick and shook her skirt. Rady stood up and went towards her. "Now see what I've done," he said, brushing at the wet skirt. "Got you all wet."

But when his hands brushed at the skirt they lingered and it was like she knew what they aimed to do. She giggled a little and pulled away, but when he followed she made no objections and let him have his way without fuss or bother. Rady remembered Annie had said she wasn't real bright, and he reckoned it must be so. But that never kept him from taking his pleasure. Nor from finding it good, either. A willing girl was a willing girl, whether she was bright or not.

When he was through he left her, saying no more to her. And he'd forgot her before he got home. The thought never once crossed his mind that he had taken out on Flary all of his feelings of the afternoon. His madness at himself for falling into the trap of his own pride. His madness at Miz Rowe for making him feel little and foolish. And his feelings of wanting to hurt and strike back at her. His feelings of hating her and wanting to make her know that it wasn't him was little and foolish, but her. Her and that sick, puling husband of hers. But mostly her. Those kind of thoughts never entered his mind. All he knew was Flary was there and willing, and taking her had been good, and that when he left her he felt like a man again.

When he got home Annie was fretted. "You been a time," she said.

"Yeah."

"Yer supper's got cold."

"I ain't hungry right now."

"Have you eat over at the Rowes'?"

Rady came close to saying he had before he thought. But Annie wouldn't of liked that. So he caught himself. "No, of course I ain't eat. I jist ain't hungry right now. I'll snack some after while."

"Well, I wisht you'd tell me when you're aimin' to miss yer supper! Hit'd save me a right smart work. The heat is bad now, to be buildin' up a big cook fire, an' then you not wantin' nothin'!"

"God's sake, Annie! A man don't allus know if he's goin' to be hungry or not. Hit'll keep, an' you got to eat yerself. Quit jawin' at me." And then he saw her eyes had filled up. "An' don't commence cryin' agin! Is yer nerves gone bad that you're allus cryin' these days? Beats all I ever seen the way you tune up over nothin'."

Annie wiped her eyes with the corner of her Sunday apron. "I wouldn't call it exactly nothin'. Livin' with you ain't allus so easy."

"How'm I different from ary other man?" Rady wanted to know. "I do my work an' git along with you as peaceable as I kin. What more kin you ask?"

Annie didn't say nothing, for there was nothing she could say without telling him what it was frashed her. How he'd gone against her renting from Mister Rowe, and the renting took him away from home and put him close to Miz Rowe. And every time he was gone longer than common it worried her for fear him and Miz Rowe were laughing and talking together, or maybe worse. Annie knew Rady too good not to worry, and if she hadn't of known him that good, she knew the ways of a ridge man. But she couldn't say so. She couldn't say that she was trying hard to have a young'un to hold him tighter, thinking, maybe, then he'd never look past her again. And she couldn't say that all of this was keeping her twitchy and nervous and easy to cry. And all Rady could make of it was that Annie was getting awful cross-grained of late.

He did up the work and when he had finished he set on the front porch and played his gittar and sung awhile. It was like he was trying to prove something to himself, for he sung "On Top of Old Smokey" twice. But at first dark he put up his gittar and went to bed. He laid there a time going over in his mind the work he had laid out to do. Tobacco had to be suckered and the corn needed plowing one more time before being laid by. In spite of the rain he'd stayed ahead, and come fall he was going to have money in his pockets. He might even buy him a good bull and commence breeding his own calves. He could run might near fifty more over on Mister Rowe's place next year. Thinking of breeding made him reach for Annie. But she was still mad with him over supper. "You've not eat yit," she told him.

"My God," he said, "you want me to git up an' eat first!"

And because she couldn't never stay mad with him very long, Annie snickered and made up with him.

When Mister Rowe got to feeling better he took his turn at having Rady learn him the gittar, but he didn't take much interest in it very long. It was just a passing fancy and it passed fast. He pestered Rady to bring him a drink now and then, and Rady made excuses when he could, and when he figured he couldn't, he took him a pint. Never more than that. He stuck to his story about the moonshiners being scared, although the hills were running likker all around. But Rady didn't want to kill off the goose that was laying the golden eggs, so he was careful about it.

And for the most part Miz Rowe stayed right friendly with Rady. But she was chancey, some days friendly and laughing, some days paying no heed to anybody. She didn't ride as hard as she'd done when they first came, for usually Mister Rowe rode out with her of an evening now, but there were still times when it was like the devil chased her and the only way she could spell him was to saddle her horse and outride him. When she was like that she was reckless and heedless and she lashed out with a quick tongue.

She came a cropper one day on account of being like that. She came out to saddle her horse and Rady could tell by one glimpse that she was feeling ugly. Her face was always pinched at those times, stiff like it had been frozen. "Get my horse," she told Rady, speaking short and sharp.

It was early for her to be riding but he didn't say nothing, just caught up her horse for her. Then he went and got the saddle while she stood and beat against her leg with the light crop she always carried when she rode. The saddle girth was tangled a mite and Rady took his time straightening it out, but Miz Rowe was of a mind not to be kept waiting. She walked over to where Rady was working on it and yanked it out of his hands. "For God's sake," she snapped at him, "must you take all day! Let me have it!" And she jerked at it and slung it over the horse and tightened it, yanking at the straps and buckles and jerking at the saddle to get it straight.

Without saying no more she swung up and cut the horse a lick that sent him tearing out towards the gate. They hadn't much more than got through the gate than Rady, who was standing watching, saw her give a lurch to one side and saw her grab at the horse's head to keep herself from falling. He knew the saddle had slipped, and it didn't surprise him none, the way she'd made haste with the girth and buckle. He saw her trying to kick her foot loose from the near stirrup, and trying to hang on while the saddle kept slipping further and further around. And the horse, scared by her grabbing and the saddle slipping and her weight hanging on one side, stopped running and commenced plunging and kicking. Rady took off on a run, but before he got there Miz Rowe sailed clean over the horse's head and landed in the bushes by the side of the road. The horse, free of his burden, lit a shuck down the road.

Rady ran as fast as he could, not knowing but what she had broken her neck falling that way, and when he come up to her she was still lying in the bushes, covered with dirt and dust. And then he saw she wasn't dead, anyways. For she was lying there, her face buried in her arms, crying. Crying hard, too, like a kid. Noisy and stormy and mad, her shoulders heaving, and while Rady was watching her feet commenced to kick in the dirt, fast and furious, raising a cloud of dust that blew away as fast as her feet stirred it up.

Rady got hold of her and tried to turn her over so's to help her up, but she twitched loose from him and dug her head down in her arms again. "Get away," she said. "Go on away and leave me alone!"

But he was afraid she was hurt, so he leaned down beside her and laid his hands on her shoulders again and tried to see her face. "You hurt, Miz Rowe? You hurt anywheres?"

She set up then and struck out at him, hitting at his hands. "I said leave me alone! Goddammit, don't you think I know how to fall? Get your filthy hands off me, Cromwell! Don't you dare touch me!"

She was screaming at him and for a minute he didn't do a thing he was so stunned. Then he got so mad he didn't even know what he was doing. He jerked her to her feet and shook her so hard her teeth chattered. "Shut up!" he yelled at her. "You shut up that bawlin' an' quit actin' like a damn fool! I ast you if you was hurt anywheres!"

She just stood there and looked at him. There was a cut on her face where she'd glanced a rock in falling, and her shirt was tore and she was all over dirty and dusty. Her hair had come loose from its ribbon and hung down over her shoulders, and it still swung a little from Rady's shaking.

"Are you hurt anywheres . . . besides that cut on yer face?" He still had hold of her shoulders, and one hand laid against the bare flesh where her shirt was tore.

She kept on staring at him, and one of her hands made a motion towards her shoulder, but she let it drop. She looked at his face like she'd never seen it before, there bent so close to her own, sweated and browned and leathered and so close she could smell the sweat and the tobacco and the dust that had settled on his eyebrows and around his nose. She looked at his hands where they laid against her shoulders. Big, broad, strong hands, squared and stoutened with years of plowing and hoeing and milking, and with a grip that could paralyze. She looked at them and she looked all down the length of his stocky, heavy body, to his feet, planted hard against the dirt. She looked and she looked, and then, as calm as a pond on a summer day, unruffled and on its surface unbetraying of any stirrings in its depths, she laid Rady's hands off her shoulders and stepped back, brushing the dust and leaves off her riding pants and straightening her shirt. "No," she said, "I'm not hurt."

Rady rubbed his hands against the sides of his pants. "Well, if yer not, it's a miracle! You could easy of broke yer neck!"

"Yes. It was very foolish of me. I was angry."

She looked around for her hair ribbon and they both had to laugh at where it was. Flung plumb over a blackberry bush and grafted to a thorn. Rady got it for her and she swung her hair back and tied it. "Thank you, Rady," she said, "I'll be more careful now."

"When you've had a fight with Mister Rowe you ortent to

ride this way. Hit's plumb foolish of you. You're liable to kill yerself."

She looked at him, straight and without flinching. "So you know."

"I ain't blind. I figgered that was what made you ride so hard. You git rid of what's bottled up in you, but it's too resky. Couldn't you git out an' walk instead?"

"Riding's better. I'm a good rider, Rady. There's no danger as long as I keep my head."

Rady laughed then. "Hit's yore head you're liable to lose you take many more falls like this'n today."

There was a quick kind of glee inside of him when she called him Rady. Oh, he took notice of it fast. And it didn't matter that she didn't know. She would know. One day, she'd know. He'd not missed the look she'd given him either. That was the beginning of the knowing. And the reaching for his hand on her shoulder. She'd screamed out at him not to touch her. Not yet knowing that's what she wanted. But she would know. And it would grow. All that fine, white proudness. All the sharp, tempered blade. All that riding of the wind. It would change . . . bend . . . lean. His way. Towards him and to him. Annie was one kind of woman. Miz Rowe was another. But all women were alike in one thing. They can be mastered. It takes one way with one kind of woman, another way with another. But in the end they bend and give to strength. They may hurt and they may weep and they may die of it. But it's like they had all of it to do, to feel the strength that causes it. That was a thing Rady knew without giving it a thought. Knew like he knew the power in his own back and legs and arms and blood. Knew because it's born in every man until he forgets it and scatters it in love. When a man loves he loses it, for he wants to please. But Rady wasn't going to love any woman enough to give her the strength to make him weak. It was Annie who had given. And it would be Miz Rowe who would give . . . in time.

That was his first knowledge of what he could have, if he so wanted it. His first glimpse of what could be turned his way. And he knew he wanted it. "I'll git yer horse," he said. "He's likely run down the road a mile or two."

Miz Rowe looked down the road, but the horse was not in sight. "All right," she said. "I'm going to the house."

Rady found the horse picking by the side of the road down by the mailboxes, and he straightened the saddle and tightened the girth and swung up astride the horse. He rode back up the road slowly, tasting what he now knew. Tasting it and liking its taste and already looking out over the fields with owning eyes. More pasture here. More corn there. More tobacco over yonder. Another barn or two. Another fifty head of beef cattle. And there was so much timber on the two places that a man had ought to do right good with a sawmill.

Like he already owned it, he rode. And like he knew this man astride his back owned him, too, the horse walked easy along the road, answering gently to the hand of the reins.

Chapter Eleven

It was in September, I reckon . . . yes, I know it was, for me and Junie were cutting tobacco, and I've yet to cut a crop before September.

I remember it was a hot, steamy day and the tobacco was higher than our heads and it was like being in a jungle to be hid down in between them close-growing stalks. Junie was cutting and I was sticking. Junie's a good hand at cutting, though she keeps a man working sharpening her blade. She won't cut a stalk with a dull edge.

We'd stopped for me to give it a turn or two and Junie was fanning herself with her bonnet, standing under the shade of a poplar tree waiting on me. Her dress was stuck to her with sweat and she kept pulling it loose to let a little breeze blow through, and I was just wondering if maybe I couldn't take a quick one, down in the field like that amongst the tobacco, when she commenced talking. "Annie's had good luck," she said, blowing down the front of her dress, "if you kin call it good luck."

"Finally took, did she?" I said, the wish beginning to pass. I'd ought to of known better anyhow. Junie's not one you can roll in the middle of the field, even if it's a lawful roll. She's got strong ideas of what's decent and proper.

The file was rasping across the blade and Junie had to raise her voice to make me hear. "Jist has," she said. "She ain't but two months gone."

"Mite soon to be shore, ain't it?" I says.

"No," Junie said, and there was some bitterness in the way she said it. "You miss twicet an' they ain't no mistakin' it."

"Junie," I says, "they's times when it appears to me you ain't so glad you ever got married!"

"Humph!" she says. "Woman marries a man all she gits is breath an' britches!"

I would of liked to remind Junie that, admitting what a woman mostly gets in a man is breath and britches, what else is there for her to marry but a man! But I never. I let it pass.

"Reckon she's right tickled," I says.

"I can't make out whether she's tickled or not. She don't act perticklerly tickled, I'd say. More like she'd done a thing she'd set out to do. More satisfied than tickled."

"Rady's not named it," I says.

"Well, of course he ain't! He don't know it yit! How would it be fer a woman to go talkin' sich things!"

It's always been a thing past understanding to me how womenfolks never let on they're in the family way. First a man knows there's another young'un on the way is when his woman's dress commences hiking up in front and her stomach commences sticking out. You'd think, him being the cause, she could name it at least to her own husband. "Hit ain't fitten," Junie tells me, her nose up in the air like I'd ought to have more sense than to wonder. It's fitten to do, but not fitten to talk about, I reckon.

I let it pass and commenced counting. Annie'd freshen, best I could figure, about April next spring. And I couldn't help sniggering over the idea it would be about the time most of the rest of the cows on Rady's place would be dropping their calves! Wondered, too, what Rady'd think when he took notice. He was likely going to be some surprised!

Rady'd been taking things slow and easy the rest of that summer, not pushing his wants or his knowledge. Just pondering and thinking and doing his work right on. And there was plenty of work to do. He kept in after the Pringles and stayed with it himself, not taking much time off for nothing. He was through cutting tobacco by the end of August, and had his corn laid by in good time.

Mister Rowe helped a little with the tobacco cutting. Not much. He came out and helped stack sticks and haul them to the barn. The heat bothered him considerable and he wasn't, to say, handy in the fields anyways. But it was more than he'd been doing to take a hand in any kind of work. Rady got along good with him, explaining like he would to a kid the right way to do things, and laughing at Mister Rowe's awkwardness. He slipped him a drink now and then, not too much or too often. Just enough to let Mister Rowe know he was his friend. Fact is, Mister Rowe got in the way more than he helped, but Rady never let on. He always took time to oversee him and made out like he was glad to have him around.

He never sought out Miz Rowe. He was polite and mannerly to her when she came around, which wasn't often at first, but he never went out of his way to look her up. He was smart, Rady was. He let her feel out her own hunger and her own knowledge, and let it drive her to him. And it did, of course.

She took to making little excuses to see him ever' once in a while, like her hunger was driving her beyond good sense. Not real often. And it would be a right smart spell in between times, like she was mad at herself for giving in to it and promising ever' time not to do it no more.

It commenced a day that was sticky after a sudden shower of rain and Rady was working in the garden patch he'd laid off for them, the ground being yet too wet to go back to the fields. She came out like she never knew he was there, and acted surprised to see him. "I came to see if the late corn was ready," she told him. "I thought I'd have some for supper if there is any. It's been quite a while since we finished the early corn, and I got hungry for some, and I . . ." She talked too fast and too hurried, her words all running together, quick and not meaning anything, flustered like a young girl coming sudden on her beau.

She had a pan with her to put the corn in, but Rady noticed

she'd put on new lipstick and had combed her hair fresh. She looked neat and clean, everything she ever put on being ironed without a wrinkle. She was always finicky about her clothes. She had on a pink dress that day . . . real pale pink, about the color of the heart of a rose, or of a baby's face when it first wakes up, flushed, from its nap. It was starched and shining from the iron and stood away from her hips like it had hoops in it. Made her waist look awful little. She wasn't so white any more either. Her skin had turned kind of a goldy color from being out in the sun . . . all over gold, even and smooth like it had been spread on with a brush and no thinning or thickening. Glisteny. She stood there with her pan in her hands, her pink skirt brushing the tops of the tomato vines, a vein in her throat beating hard against the smooth gold skin, and her black hair tied back with a ribbon the same pink of her dress. And the sun, hazy from the rain, was still strong enough to bring out the red in her hair. And she was as fair as a picture drawn by a master hand.

But for all her pink and black and gold prettiness, and for all her coming to the garden had made Rady want to laugh with something high and fine in his throat springing up—for all of that, he acted like it was nothing. Acted polite and mannerly and anxious to get what she wanted. "Best let me git it fer you," he told her. "Them corn bees kin sting pretty keen. Yore arms is naked, an' they'll swarm all over 'em in no time."

He looked at her arms then, and like what he'd said had a special meaning to her, she looked at them too and then she pulled at the short sleeves which reached just to the elbow. "Ort to wear long sleeves when you come in the garden," Rady said.

He took the pan and went over to the far side of the garden where the corn was growing, and she stood where she was and waited. Had he looked back he could of seen her watching him, big-shouldered, stout-necked, flat-hipped, and he could of seen the little shudder that ran all over her before she took her eyes off of him. But he never needed to look back, and wouldn't of. He knew she was looking, and he knew what he looked like to her. A man. All man. One that could take care of her any day she said so. And would. And he knew she was scared to death of her own self. And that as scared as she was, she was wanting him worse than she was afraid. She was commencing to bend . . . and he allowed she'd break inside another couple of months. If his luck held. And he aimed to see it held.

He pulled a dozen ears and brought them back to her. "They's not many ready yit," he said, "but I reckon these'll make you a mess."

She took the pan and when she took it, Rady let his hand touch hers, just in passing. Not really to say touching. Just kind of brushing, like a butterfly tips an open flower, dip and brush, so light it's more like a flutter than anything else. Just his fingers brushed over her hand, like it was an accident, like it was nothing to him, like it had no meaning at all.

But when he touched her she jerked the pan away from him and the corn spilled out at their feet. She ducked her head, but not before he had seen her swallow hard, and not before he'd seen the pupils of her eyes widen to show how quick her heart had beat up fast. And there was a kind of glory inside him to know what she was feeling . . . a leaping, springing kind of glory that could of shouted and sung and strutted his own power and man-ness. But he gave no sign of it. Not a muscle moved, nor an eyelash quivered, nor even the pull of smile at the corner of his mouth. He picked up the corn and put it back in the pan and she turned around and walked away from him, stumbling like she couldn't see where she was going. "You're trampling the cucumber vines," Rady told her, and though he spoke but little above a whisper, her shoulders jerked and she pulled her feet back on the path again.

Like he'd looked into her eyes he knew they were blind with wetness. He watched her hips swaying down the path as she went around the vines and plants, and he thought of her without the pink dress . . . her hips swaying . . . and like the dress had dropped from around her, he could see her, white where the gold of the sun left off, and he could of buried himself and died in that whiteness. He turned around of a sudden and heaved a big rock over on its side. Just to be lifting a heavy weight and so ease the tightness inside him. It wasn't so easy to wait. But it was worth waiting for. All of it was worth waiting for, and there were rocks to heave aplenty, and there was always Annie and the big double bed at home.

Better than two weeks went by then before Miz Rowe came around him again. She rode out to the far field where he was working, along about the middle of the afternoon, with a half-gallon fruit jar full of cold lemonade. She said nothing when she rode up, nor nothing when she handed it to him. No reason nor explanation. She just rode out where he was, handed him the lemonade and set there on her horse and listened to him talk and watched him drink it. "Mighty nice of you to think of this. Miz Rowe," Rady told her. "Hit goes good on a hot day like today."

She made him no answer, just looked at him like there wasn't no use her saying a word. Like the offering of the lemonade was a sign itself that the long, loose wire that stretched between her and Rady was tightening and had brought her, unwilling, where he was. Like it was, maybe, a sign of another offering she was commencing to know she was going to make. And like she was studying herself and Rady to know why.

She set there a time, saying nothing, looking at him and listening to him. Of a sudden she broke into what he was saying. "What is your wife like?"

It surprised Rady some. "Annie? Why, I don't know . . . you mean what does she look like? Ain't you never seen her?"

"No."

"Well, whyn't you come over sometime an' git acquainted. It ain't fur over there. She'd make you welcome."

"No."

Like he could see inside her he knew then she'd been thinking of him and Annie together, and it had been tormenting her. She had to know if Annie was pretty and young and if Rady was crazy about her. But she didn't want to see for herself.

"Well, I don't know as I kin tell you about her," Rady said. "Allus hard fer me to tell what anybody looks like. Annie's kind of short an' plump, kind of round . . . jist a right nice armful," he grinned. "She's got kind of crinkly curly hair, an' she's right pretty. We ain't been married but a little better'n two years . . ." he said the last kind of shy, left it hanging in the air, like a man who hadn't been married but a couple of years still found it so good he was a little bashful to be talking about it. What he left unsaid spoke more than what he said. It drew a picture of a pretty, plump woman, a right nice armful to love, and the newness of loving her still on him. That was the way it sounded. And Rady left it sounding that way. Adding nothing to it. So the words would stay, dull and blunt, not to be rid of, and to be heard over and over again. To be lived with and eaten and tasted. To hone the edge of want like a whetstone against a knife blade. To sharpen and thin and shine . . .

Miz Rowe looked at Rady leaning against the tree where he'd stepped into the shade while he drank. She watched him lift the jar to his mouth, and she saw his throat swallowing, and she saw the way his hand, broad and brown, closed around the jar, and the way his shirt sleeve rolled back from his wrist and left the yellow, bleached hairs strong and wiry on the leather of his arm. Like the turn of his wrist, and the bleached wiry hairs, and the span of his hand were a snake to charm, she looked at them. And then she pulled her horse around and rode back across the field. She rode slow, but she set as straight in the saddle as she'd ever done, even though the clopping of the horse's hoofs were like the words she'd heard being tramped steady and heavy against her ears, and the remembrance of the brown throat and hand and wrist was tied to the words, like a sickness jailed in the body, heaving and pitching, but not getting free. The throat and the hand and the wrist went with the pretty, plump woman, knew her and their pleasure of her . . . night after night after night.

Chapter Twelve

Miz Rowe had a pride that served her well and she called it up to serve her now. She quit making up piddling little excuses to seek Rady out after that. She quit trying to shun him. What ever it cost her to do it, she went back to her old way of seeing him around when it came easy or natural. She quit hiding behind Mister Rowe of an evening when she wanted to ride, or waiting for Rady to go home. When Mister Rowe wasn't in a notion to ride with her, she went out, like always, whether Rady was around or not, and caught up her horse, or had him to, and rode. When Rady was at the house, talking to Mister Rowe, she listened or joined in with her own ideas. It was like she had made up her mind to something and had hewed her a course.

Rady was just finishing up cutting the tobacco on the Rowe place, with his own still to cut, when Mister Rowe got sick. It commenced with him going on a rip-snorting toot one night along about the middle of the week. Rady'd been home and in bed long enough to be sound asleep when the dogs waked him up, barking. They were making a right smart fuss so he figured it must be a stranger, and he slipped into his overhalls and went out to the front porch to see. He didn't light a lamp. A careful man's not going to show himself to a stranger.

"Dammit, get down!" he heard somebody say, and he grinned in the dark. It was Miz Rowe. And then she called. "Rady! Rady Cromwell!"

"Somethin' wrong, Miz Rowe?" he answered and went out to the gate to make the dogs shut up.

"Jim's got a real load on and he's out of hand. He's tearing up the place and I can't do a thing with him."

"Wait'll I dress," Rady told her, and he went back in the house.

Annie had waked and was up making a light when he went in the bedroom. "What is it?" she asked.

"Hit's Miz Rowe. Mister Rowe's on a tear an' she can't do nothin' with him. I got to go."

"At this time of night?" Annie peered to look at the clock, her eyes still half-shut with sleep. "Why, it's nigh onto midnight!"

"What difference does it make what time of night it is? If he's crazy drunk he's crazy drunk, an' she's skeered."

"Oh, shore," Annie sniffed, mad even at the mention of Miz Rowe's name. "When she crooks her little finger, you got to go!"

Rady didn't bother to answer, just went on dressing, and he went out without saying more to her. He was puzzled where Mister Rowe had got the likker, him not having give him any, but Miz Rowe told him a fellow had been down from the city all day, man Mister Rowe had gone to college with, and that he brought it.

Him and Miz Rowe struck out in a hurry, her telling him what had happened as they went along. "I knew he and Tom were drinking a little all day," she said, "but I never dreamed Jim had had enough to make him drunk. It usually makes him sick before then. When Tom left, I went for a ride and I got back just before dark. I meant to have dinner at once, but when I walked into the kitchen Jim was standing there in the middle of the floor, throwing plates at a target he'd drawn on the wall!"

Rady couldn't keep from laughing, and she kind of laughed a little herself. It was funny, Mister Rowe standing there solemn as an owl, heaving dishes at a big red bull's eye he'd drawn on the white painted wall. But it hadn't stayed funny. She'd tried to quiet him down and he'd just got worse, going hog-wild, breaking up the furniture and stomping around all over the place, threatening her and yelling he'd kill anybody tried to come close, like there was a whole army trying to get him. She hadn't really got scared though till he commenced looking for the key to his gun cabinet. He'd forgot where he put it, but with a drunkard's luck she figured he'd run across it, and with a gun in his hands he'd be a dangerous man. That was when she'd decided to come get Rady.

When they got there Mister Rowe was still rampaging around, cussing up a storm, looking for his key. Rady tried talking to him, begging him to go to bed, promising to find his key for him, pleading with him, but he couldn't do a thing with him. So finally he told Miz Rowe, "I don't know nothin' to do but knock him out."

"Go ahead," she said, as cool as a cucumber.

Rady cornered him and put him to sleep with a haymaker where it did the most good. Then he undressed him and put him to bed and went on home.

He allowed, that'd be all there was to it, saving Mister Rowe would be upchucking all the next day. And he was, but instead of getting better then, he just kept on getting sicker and sicker. Wouldn't nothing stay on his stomach, and in a couple of days he'd quit trying to put anything into it. And he was nearabouts crazy with pains in his head and stomach and legs.

It went on for three or four days, then Miz Rowe went out to the barn where Rady was racking the last of the tobacco. "Rady," she said, "he's not getting over this one. He's awfully sick, and I think we'd better get him to a hospital. Where's the closet one?"

"The city, I reckon . . . Louisville." Rady left the tobacco and crawled down from the tiers.

They decided for Rady to go into town, the little county seat town twenty miles away, and make the arrangements to get Mister Rowe to the city. He was too sick to go in a car, even if the Rowes or Rady had had one, so they thought to take him on the train. But they had to get him to the train one way or the other. The town didn't have an ambulance, so finally Rady hit on the idea of having the funeral home send the hearse out after him.

Sick as he was that tickled Mister Rowe till he laughed himself
into another heaving spell. "Jim, shut up!" Miz Rowe told him.

"Well, by God," he said, still laughing, "I'll bet I'm the first
man ever took a hearse ride and knew it! I'll find out how it feels
to be a corpse. Only a corpse doesn't feel, does it?"

"Don't be morbid! I said shut up!"

"I'm not being morbid. I just think it's funny."

"Well, I don't."

She went with him to the city and stayed several days, but
him being an alcoholic as well as the other things was wrong
with him, they wouldn't even let her see him, so after a while she
came on back home.

While she was gone Rady'd finished up on the Rowe place.
The corn was laid by, the tobacco cut and racked in the barn, and
everything was tidy so's the Pringles would only have to keep an
eye on things and could turn to cutting and sawing up the winter
wood. Work was pressing on Rady's place, though. He went over
the day Miz Rowe came home to ask after him, but he set to then
cutting his own tobacco and getting caught up around the place.
Must of been a week or ten days he never even went near the
Rowe place. Then he went over late one evening just to take a
look around and make sure the old man and boys were keeping
busy. He satisfied himself they were doing all right and then he
went over towards the house to ask after Mister Rowe again.

Miz Rowe saw him coming across the back lot and met him
near the gate. "Where have you been?" she said, her mouth as
tight-crimped as if she'd been his wife.

"Workin' over at home," he says, "why?"

"You didn't say you weren't coming . . . you didn't tell me . . . I
didn't know . . ."

"Why would I tell you? I'm caught up here, an' I've not slacked
nothin'. The Pringles is takin' keer of what's to do."

"I didn't mean you'd neglected anything."

He knew what she meant. She'd looked for him every day
and he hadn't come. And every day he hadn't come she'd looked
that much longer and that much harder the next day, getting
more and more uneasy and restless. He knew how the days had

gone, with her standing at the back door keeping her eye on the woods path, watching for him and looking to see him come through the gate. Getting mad at herself for being so foolish and flinging herself around to do some chore in the house, and fifteen minutes later taking up her stand at the door, unable to keep busy at anything for fear she'd miss him. Like he'd been there, he could see her, fixing her breakfast and pulling the table over so's she could keep an eye on the gate while she ate. Then she'd wash the dishes, watching out the window. She'd string out her kitchen chores as long as she could, because she could see the gate from the kitchen. But finally, and he yet hadn't come, she'd have the other rooms to redd up, and he knew how she'd make up half the bed, maybe, before giving in to the need to go to the kitchen door. And she would stand a few minutes, then cuss a little maybe, and maybe cry a little, and go back and make up the other side of the bed. He knew how it had been, with her vowing to herself she wouldn't watch the gate, and breaking her vow five minutes later. He knew well enough what she had meant when she came out to the back gate, her mouth crimped and her words short.

"Don't you think," she said, "it would have been nicer to tell me you were going to work at home this week?"

"I don't know," Rady said. "I never thought what was nice or what wasn't. I never thought it was any of yore business one way or the other. I ain't a perticklerly nice feller, Miz Rowe."

"You certainly are not!" she stormed out at him. "Well, now that you're here, will you saddle up for me?"

"Why, shore," and he went in the barn to get her saddle.

She watched him go into the barn, and then she flung around and went into the house to change her clothes. When she came out Rady had her horse ready for her. She got on and pulled the horse's head around like she was leaving. Then she pulled him up and looked down at Rady. "Ride with me," she said. "Get Jim's horse and ride with me."

Rady made as if to look at the saddle girth. He had to move her foot out of the way, and he was slow turning loose of her ankle. He looked up at her and said, kind of soft, "I couldn't do that, Miz Rowe. Hit would be all over the settlement in less'n an hour that we'd been ridin' together, with him gone. Hit wouldn't do."

She bit her lip and he could tell she was close to crying.

"But I tell you," he went on, "I'll wait fer you in the woods. Down by the branch."

"No," she said, quick-like, "no!"

"All right. But I'll wait. An' I'll be there this time of evenin' ever' day. I'll be there when you want to come."

He figured there wasn't much use him waiting that evening, but he did so, until nearly dark. She didn't come. And she didn't come the next day nor the next. But she did come finally, of course. He'd known she would. All he had to do was wait.

She came from the house, in a white dress like a bride's, and she was crying when she came. Rady saw her stop at the gate and look back at the house, and then duck her head and hurry into the woods. He went to meet her, his hair still wet from the bath he'd taken in the brook. He was always clean with his body, but in the summertime he was downright finicky, going to the creek every evening to wash himself of the sweat and field dust. His clothes now were the ones he'd had on all day, but under them his body was clean and ready.

He went to meet her and she came straight to him, not making a sound with her crying, just letting the tears roll unhindered down her face. But even with her face wet with tears there was still a look of pride on it. She didn't come gladly, nor she didn't even come willingly, but she did come pridefully.

And she went straight into Rady's arms like a homing pigeon, fierce and eager and hungry. Hill men don't talk at such times. They don't make love by talkin'; they just take, and even if Rady had wanted to talk, he knew she wouldn't. She'd come . . . she was ready. He held her, and like they were one body they touched and pressed and flattened, melting together in the hardness of their touching. Like a waterdry deer, they slaked the long thirst of their mouths, drinking deep and greedy, until neither of them had any breath left. Like starved pieces of living flesh seeking food, their hands and their mouths looked for and found the places of love, neither of them saying a word, neither of them even knowing when they sank down to the bed of moss on the bank of the brook. All they knew was, it was now . . . the joining and the finishing of what they had started. They were shaking with the need, impatient of the end. They didn't even take off their clothes that first time. It wasn't that Rady took her . . . they took each other, she matching his heat with her own, following him in the mounting rhythm, in the hurried sweeping away of all things real and solid, completely joined, one flesh. Followed him, or led him, into the quick breathing, the quivering, shivering suns and shaking earth, until the dam was broken . . . the flood spilled.

Not even afterwards did they talk much. Once Miz Rowe moved her head on the moss and Rady took off his shirt and made a pillow for her. "You'll be cold," she said.

"No."

She looked around her at the woods. "It's a pretty place."

"Yes."

She slid her hand into a flat band of sunlight and turned it this way and that to watch the light, studying it. The back of her hand was smooth and gold . . . and then she turned her hand over and made a cup of it. She held the sunlight in the cup of her hand, and then she opened her fingers and spilled it out, slow, like she had used it up and it was no good to her now. She turned her head to look at Rady.

"Is the sun almost down?"

"Almost."

He turned over on his stomach and laid his face on his folded arms, so he could look at her. He was bare above the waist and she put out her hand and ran a finger down his back. He shivered.

She smiled at him and took her hand away.

He smiled back at her and then he closed his eyes and slept a little. Not long, for the sun was still tipping the trees when he woke. But he didn't know when she had left. There was only a little flattening of the moss where she had laid, and his shirt was still warm from her head.

Chapter Thirteen

Rady never made the mistake of acting like Miz Rowe was beholding to him. He took no advantage of that evening in the woods. Never presumed on it at all. Most guys would of. Would of been clumsy enough to have taken for granted that once would guarantee more. But Rady didn't. He never acted like there'd be other times, or even another time. He knew Miz Rowe pretty good by now. Before, where he had made her know what she could have, by touching her and reminding her of her own wants, he now left her free to remind herself by her own remembering. He acted like he had never touched her. Like he didn't know how she'd come in a white dress with tears running down her face. Like he didn't know how greedy and starved and hungry she'd been. Like he didn't know how the bed of moss was barely flattened where she'd lain.

And he did it without making her feel it had been quick done and over for him, forgot and moved on past. That would have made her feel as cheap as pestering and reminding would have made her sick. He didn't make that mistake.

Instead he made her know the shine was all there, and he did it by going about his business as usual, only adding one thing. In little ways he took more care of her and consideration. At best, with plenty of money, living in the backwoods has got a lot of everyday problems. And the Rowes never had plenty of money now. Long since they had had to send the people they'd brought with them back to the city. They had no help of any kind about the house. And while there were conveniences in their house most ridge folks would of counted luxuries, they burned wood for heat and cooking just like the rest of us, and Miz Rowe did the washing and tended the house like any other woman in the settlement. She had the electric in the house, and she had a washing machine. And she had a hand pump in the kitchen to furnish her water. But it wasn't easy for a woman used to city ways and the ways of money. There were lots of ways Rady could make things easier for her. Like getting her wash water ready for her the night before. Like separating the milk before it was brought in the house. Like seeing her firewood was good burning and stacked handy to use. And he did so. And every extra thing he did was like telling her she was fine and good and nice, and to be cared for and protected.

He did those extra things as casual as the regular work, made no fuss or bother with them, and saw to it they laid no pressure on her. Saving the pressure of her own wants, stirred by the sight of him day after day.

There were other times, of course. But Rady let them come at her wish. Like he knew that was the only way they could come without tearing down something in her that held her together. But like he'd done when he told her he'd wait in the woods till she came, he gave her the feeling that he was always waiting. Like all she had to do was pick her own time and place and he'd be there, waiting.

She never would say a time and place, though. She never would say, "I'll meet you this evening," or pick a time ahead, or name a place. She would come, instead, of a sudden, like something inside her had, right then, to be fed and satisfied, without waiting.

It suited Rady. It was a man's way and he could understand it. A thing planned and named has none of the need that must be met now, and loses by its naming and planning some of its goodness. He liked it in her. And besides it gave him a feeling of excitement. He never knew ahead what day, or what hour she'd seek him out.

She met him twice more at the same place in the woods before Mister Rowe came home. Without saying anything to him, she would be there in the evening when he cut through on his way home. Waiting where the path turned by the brook and where the moss laid heavy on the bank. And it was like it had been the first time . . . hard and greedy and hungry. No words said. Just a starved, needful joining.

Then when Mister Rowe came home, white and weak and shaky, and housebound by the first chilly days of October, she came to the barn one rainy afternoon, and they climbed to the hayloft. It was good up there, high up in the barn with the hay warm and sweet-smelling all around them, and the rain solid and heavy on the roof right over their heads. She was different that afternoon. She was more free, less greedy, less knotted up. It was like the rain and the nest of hay and the gray day had soothed her somehow, making her slip some tight hold inside, and by slipping the tight hold, let her take with a kind of gladness, and give with a joyfulness Rady had not known in her before. It was like she knew, all at once, it was more than the hard, starved need. Like she knew, now, it was fun . . . play . . . laughing . . . talking.

That was the first time she took her clothes off, and she did it quick and in a hurry, without Rady's asking or his help, like she wanted to be shut of them and unhindered. She laughed when she saw the mat of hair on Rady's chest and buried her face in it and bit him, easy at first and then hard, until he swore at her and cuffed her loose from him. They laughed a lot that afternoon, and slept a little and woke and laughed again, at the hay in their hair, at the wrinkles it made on their bodies, at the itch it made on their backs, and they were together again, still laughing, teasing and loving all together.

The hayloft was where they were together after that. It was too cold and too rainy for outdoors, and besides they liked it there. Maybe the hay was like the twigs and straw and bits of string a bird uses to build a nest with. Maybe the loft, being high in the barn, was like the top of a tree. Anyway, they liked it, and once a week maybe, or every ten days or so that fall and early winter Miz Rowe came to the barn and waited for Rady. He knew when she was there. She left her red ribbon hanging on a nail at the foot of the ladder.

Sometimes she'd be asleep when he went up to her, curled up like a little girl in a bed of hay, and he'd wake her by tickling her neck with a straw, or by kissing her so soft she'd brush like it was a gnat or moth. Sometimes she'd be reading, and maybe she'd pretend she hadn't heard him coming and not put her book aside until he snatched it away. Sometimes she was happy and ready to laugh and tease. Sometimes she was broody and cried easy. Sometimes she talked a blue streak, fast and hurried, and sometimes she was quiet and made Rady do the talking.

However it was with her, though, during those fall and first winter days, during the time of the falling of leaves, and of the shucking of corn, and of the shortening of days, she never talked about one thing. It was like she had agreed with herself not to name it. Like she was afraid, maybe, to mention it or look straight at it or handle it at all. She never talked about what they were going to do. She never said what's to come of this, or where is it going, or what will be its end. She never said to Rady, what are we going to do? She never said, what about Annie? And she surely never said, what about Jim? It was like she'd called a truce with time and was trying to get him to settle for Now. Like this time, this gray, misty day in the hayloft, was all there was. No more to come. Nothing real beyond it. This, now, was all. And she never talked about more.

Rady never named it, for he knew there would be more. He hadn't yet thought it out, and I wouldn't say for sure he ever did. I misdoubt but few men, looking back on their lives, would say I did this and this and this because I knew what I wanted and where I was going. Instead he'd say I did this because a thing came up I could turn my way. And I did that because it came handy. And I did this other thing because it happened so. And then put them all together and you can see how a man always does what's in his nature to do. And he goes where it's his nature to go, and he wants what's in his nature to want. Once Rady wanted a gun, and he got it. He wanted a dog, and he got it. He wanted a gittar, and he got that too. They were in his nature to want, and he followed his nature. Then he wanted Annie and Harm Abbott's farm. It turned out he could work it his way. Now he wanted Miz Rowe and the Rowe place. He didn't know yet how he would get them, but he never doubted for a minute that he would. For besides it being his nature to want certain things, it was his nature also to get what he wanted.

There was time, though, and he rode it easy, content to wait, to let something come up, to let something turn handy, to let something happen. He'd know when it did.

Tobacco market opens the first week in December and Rady was right there with his loads, one in Mister Rowe's name, one in his own. And when it sold and he got his checks he went to the bank and cashed his own. Mister Rowe's he endorsed and put in the bank like he'd been told. When he got home that night he set down and did some figuring. He'd sold fifteen yearlings that fall and twelve hogs. He had a fine tobacco crop of his own, and half of Mister Rowe's due him. Even after taking out what he owed old man Pringle he'd made a good profit. He figured he had enough he could get the bull he wanted, and with Mister Rowe furnishing the land and the seed for another pasture, it wouldn't cost him much to raise a bigger herd next year. He could buy, say, ten more calves and raise ten of his own, breed Mister Rowe's cows and take half the calves and market anyway forty head. He'd have to clear some new land and raise more corn, but there was land aplenty, and he'd see that it made corn a plenty. His mind was sharp and clear, thinking straight and seeing it all work out.

He went over to Mister Rowe's the next day and laid all his figures in front of him. To give him credit, Rady never cheated a penny on Mister Rowe. He had receipts for all his business and he turned them over to him along with every dime that was coming to him. But of course it looked right scant to a man that was used to alot. He kind of made a wry face when he looked at the statements. "That all?" he said.

"Hit's pretty good, Mister Rowe," Rady told him. "We got a fair price on the tobaccer, an' the extry corn an' oats. We done right good seems to me."

Mister Rowe handed the statements to Miz Rowe. "That's what we'll have to live on another year."

She looked at them. "I don't imagine we'll go to Florida for the winter this year," she said, and she kind of laughed.

"Had you been thinkin' of sich?" Rady asked.

"Don't be silly!" she said.

Mister Rowe laughed then. "Cordelia's sense of humor takes an ironical turn occasionally," he said. "We used to spend all our winters in Florida." He said it flat and even. Like it was so far past he could scarcely remember. Like it was so done with there was no use remembering. But there was a kind of homesickness in the words anyhow.

Miz Rowe looked at him quiet and funny, and her mouth crimped a little, but she never said nothing. She just got up suddenly and left the room.

Rady'd been waiting for her to go so he could tell Mister Rowe about his intentions of buying the bull. He explained what he aimed to do. "We kin raise a lot more beef thataway," he said. "I kin pasture him an' feed him this winter, but we'll have to clear some of yore land come spring an' seed more pastures to take keer of a bigger herd."

Mister Rowe just nodded his head. "Go ahead. Whatever you like. If it'll make us any more money, go ahead."

So Rady bought him a fine, white-faced bull. It stirred up a right smart excitement, and all the menfolks in the settlement drifted around to take a look at him. He was a big-shouldered animal, weighty and powerful-looking, and about as mean-tempered a critter as ever I saw. Rady had him in the little pasture next the barn.

"You goin' to strengthen this fence, ain't you?" I asked him the day I went over to look at the animal.

"Yeah," he said, "when I kin get to it."

"Better git to it soon," I said, "hit don't look none too stout to hold that critter."

But he was sure a fine-looking animal, and it was going to be right handy having a bull on the ridge. Save us taking the cows plumb across the holler to old man Smith's place. I allowed we'd get a little better strain of calves, too.

Junie was splitting cook wood when I got home, me having gone off and forgot to fill the wood box. She handed me the axe and the tight way she was holding her mouth I reckoned it would of been a pleasure to her to sink it to the helve in my brains. If she would of give me credit for having any.

"Where you been?" she said.

"Over to Rady's," I said.

"Lookin' at that brute, I reckon."

Not even to me would Junie of used the word bull. I don't know why a woman thinks brute is nicer, seeing as they both mean the same animal. But they do.

"You see Annie?" Junie said when I got the wood split.

"I never went inside," I said, "Why?"

"Jist wonderin' if she's showin' yit. I've not seen her in a right smart spell."

"How far along is she now?"

Junie counted on her fingers. "Near six months, I reckon."

"You wouldn't have to see her to know she's showin', then, seems to me."

"I dunno. Annie's kind of chunky. Them kind goes right up to the last without showin' much. Not like me. Take a beanpole like me an' I allus look like a orange in the middle of a stockin'."

"What difference does it make?" I says, "Whether she shows soon or late, or looks like a sack of meal or a orange in the middle of a stockin'. Woman's got a kid inside her has got one, an' one thing is sure as gospel. It can't be hid but nine months."

Junie just looked at me over an armload of wood. There wasn't no use her saying a word. The way she looked at me said enough. That men, and me especially, were the damndest fools God ever created and how a woman put up with them was more than she could understand! Then she turned around and marched herself into the house, her back as stiff as a ramrod.

Rady never stoutened his fence in time. He was in a hurry to get his winter wheat sowed and he allowed he'd get that done first before commencing to mend fences. The bull had broke out twice, on the far side, and Annie was plumb provoked with him.

"I wisht," she told Rady, "you'd git to that fence! That brute's goin' to git loose some day an' do some damage."

It hadn't set none too good with her for Rady to get the critter. Anything that tied him up at all with the Rowes, she was against. And she hated the bull from the day Rady brought him home.

"I'm aimin' to," Rady said. "Jist got a couple more days work. I'm aimin' to git good, stout hog wire an' fence him in."

"He gits loose in my winter turnips an' I'll take a scantlin' to him!" Annie warned. "I'll bust his old mean head in fer him!"

"You stay away from him," Rady said. "He's ill-tempered an' mean."

"I ain't askeered of him," Annie said, kind of scornful-like. And she wasn't. She wasn't never afraid of animals of no kind.

"Jist the same," Rady told her, "you stay away from him. Mind."

They'd been eating dinner and he went on back outside. He was sowing wheat on his own tobacco patch that day, not far from the house. Just a whoop and a holler away. He stopped by the barn for a little drink and then went back to his work. He allowed he'd finish up the tobacco patch that afternoon.

He hadn't been back at work more than an hour, though, till he heard Annie screaming for him, and he dropped the seeder and went tearing out across the patch towards the house. He had to cut through a little draw where the spring was at, and then up the slope to get to the house. He couldn't see on account of the rise in the ground until he got plumb to the top.

Annie was still screaming for him. The bull had broke out, this time on the near side of the pasture, and had got into her winter turnips just like she'd feared. She had a board might nigh as big as her, waving at him, and she was shooing her apron at him, and all the time screaming as loud as *she* could. The bull was pawing the ground and snorting and tromping around. Rady yelled at her but she was making so much noise herself she never heard him.

The worst thing she could have of done, of course, was to shoo her apron and scream like she was doing. That just excited the bull that much more. Had she gone in the garden and made no noise and just whacked him over the rump, likely she could of chased him back into the pasture. But she was mad and she was doing what a woman thinks of first to do. Shoo and scream.

Rady never had to say much for me to see the whole thing just like it happened: him, running for all he was worth, watching Annie dodging around, screaming and whacking at the bull, trying to make her hear him telling her to quit and cut and run for it. Before he ever got anywhere near the garden fence the bull charged, but he said Annie got out of the way. She was so mad, though, that she hit the beast on the rump as he went past, which only maddened him more so that he turned and charged again. I reckon a lot of Annie's dislike for the brute was behind her fighting him that way. Not ever having taken to him, feeling like she did that he was one more tie to the Rowes, when she found him in her turnips she must of just boiled over and lost her head. It sure wasn't a sensible thing to do to walk inside that garden patch with a board and commence beating the critter with it.

Rady said when the bull charged at her the second time she acted like she'd come to her senses and commenced running for the gate; only the animal got between her and it, so she took off towards the back side of the garden. That was where Rady was the closest. He'd come from the field across the draw and up the slope on the back side. Annie saw him coming and she swerved towards him. She never made it.

Seeing Rady she commenced screaming again and motioning towards the bull, which wasn't more than six foot behind her, purely blowing his breath down her neck. Rady said he was winded from running up the draw, but he was churning his legs for all they was worth, and he wasn't more than twenty foot from the fence, shouting and yelling ever' step. That was when he had the bad luck to stumble into a mole run, and the soft dirt give way underneath his foot and he went down, creening his ankle. He said it was when he felt his foot turning that he thought now it would be all over . . . nothing could save her now. And for a minute he had a feeling of its being meant to be. With Annie gone . . . it flashed into and across his mind that with Annie gone nothing but Mister Rowe stood between him and that fine farm, and Mister Rowe was a sick man. With Annie gone he'd still have

all he'd ever had with her, and he'd be free to get the rest. Miz
Rowe . . . the house, the timber, the acres. The picture of them
rose up before him, easier to get now, closer to him and almost
where he could reach out and take hold.

But he heard Annie scream again and he struggled up and
ran on, stumbling on account of his ankle hurting. He had to look
at the end of it, no way of not seeing it. The bull gored her from
the back, lifting her up and throwing her, and then she went
down, screaming, turning, trying pitifully to protect the baby,
her two hands covering and shielding. The animal was on top of
her in a second, though, cutting with his hooves, digging and
trompling, goring her and lifting and throwing her, then pawing
and trompling again. It sure must of been a terrible thing to see.

Rady grabbed a bracing pole in the fence corner and climbed
the fence. On the other side he used the pole to prod and poke at
the beast till he had it distracted from Annie, then he ran him off
into the barn lot. Annie was still alive when he got back to her
and he said she kept trying to crawl away, kept trying to protect
her stomach with her arms, rolling, inching away. He picked her
up and started to the house with her, sick to his stomach at the
sight of her. She was already gone when he got there with her.
He laid her on the bed, he said, and went outside and puked.

Me and Junie went as fast as we could when we heard, and
Junie helped wash Annie and lay her out. She wasn't very nice to
look at. Broke and crumpled and cut to pieces. Junie said she
was one of the worst corpses she'd ever tended. But they did the
best they could for her and when they'd finished and fixed up the
bed nice she looked a heap better.

I was setting by the fire with Rady when they called him.
"You kin come look at her now, Rady."

And I went in with him to stand by him. "She looks real
natural, don't she?" Junie said.

Rady nodded his head. "You all done good," he said, "an' I'm
much obleeged."

Then the womenfolks set about to fix supper and me and
Rady set down by the fire again. "Rady," I said, "don't grieve too
hard. You done all you could."

He looked up from the fire. "I reckon so. If I'd not fell into that mole run I might of got there in time . . ."

"An' you might not of. You couldn't help that mole run being where it was at, noway."

"No." He kind of shuddered, and I knew he was seeing it all over again.

"You got any likker?" I asked him, thinking a big drink would be the best thing for him right then, and to tell the truth I needed one myself.

"Out to the barn," he said.

So we went out to the barn and got the jug down and took ourselves several good big drinks. The likker was fiery and raw, but it set good on the stomach. Especially when a man's stomach was a mite queasy anyhow. Loosened your guts and made you feel easier. When we'd nearly emptied it Rady started to set the jug back up in the hay. It come over me then, and I said, "You kin keep yer jug in the house now, if you want. There won't be no woman to mind."

Rady turned and looked at it, and rubbed his hand down the side of it, then he kind of grinned. "Reckon I better not git out of the habit."

If he'd said so his meaning couldn't of been plainer. He was aiming to have Miz Rowe.

We went back in the house and out of respect for Annie, set up the balance of the night. It was a long night. A watch with a corpse always is. But I will say for Rady that he never once closed his eyes.

Chapter Fourteen

I reckon the first time Miz Rowe had ever laid eyes on Annie was the day she came over to see her a corpse. There wasn't any flowers to be had, it being wintertime, but she'd picked some green vines, ivy I reckon it was, and made a kind of wreath of it, and she brought it along. Junie was there, and several other women of the settlement. Junie said Miz Rowe never said much. Just went in to look at Annie in the casket and laid her vines on it. It was Junie took her in to see her, and she said Miz Rowe looked at her a long time. Never shed a tear like most feeling people would of done. Just looked, and stood there white as a ghost, until Junie got afraid maybe she was kind of sick. Some folks can't stand to look on death, and Junie didn't know but what Miz Rowe was like that.

Rady was in the fireplace room when she came out, but she never spoke to him at all. Didn't, as far as Junie could tell, even so much as look at him. Junie misdoubted Miz Rowe had any great liking for Rady, but the whole settlement thought it kindly of her to come look at Annie. She never went to the funeral, but seeing as she'd already been as mannerly as she was called on to be, nobody faulted her none for that.

Nobody knew, of course, of the meeting between her and Rady the next day after the funeral, when she had cried and cried and cried in Rady's arms, not able to tell him why, and not able to stop. He'd held her until she got hold of herself and could talk. "I hated her," she said, "until I saw her. Looked down on her lying there dead and still and gone. And then I loved her. It was like we were the same woman, loving and caring and feeling. And it was like part of me lay there, in her, dead and gone past caring. And part of her was in me, still alive, to keep on living and caring. Both being hurt by the same things. Both being hurt by you . . . and you not caring! And I hated you!"

"Why would you say I hurt you both?" Rady said, puzzled-like. "I never hurt Annie that I know of. I wouldn't of, knowingly. I allus done the best I could by her. An' I wouldn't hurt you, neither."

Miz Rowe stared at him. "You don't really know, do you? You honestly don't know!"

"Know what?"

"That just by being yourself you hurt!"

"What is a man goin' to be but hisself?"

Miz Rowe laughed. "Nothing. Nothing at all. And a woman just has to go on being hurt." She was quite a time before she went on. "They say she was going to have a baby."

"I never knew that," Rady said.

"No. You probably didn't. But it wouldn't have stopped you, would it?"

"Stopped me from what?"

"From . . . from us . . ."

Rady never knew what she wanted him to say, but he told her the truth. "No," he said, "wouldn't nothin' on God's green earth of stopped me . . . from us." He waited a minute and watched her. He couldn't tell from her face what she was thinking. "Would you of wanted it to?"

Her mouth twisted. "I wish I could say I would have. I wish I were that kind of person. Honest and clean and honorable. No, you crazy, damn fool! I wouldn't have wanted it to stop you! I would have hurt her as much as you would have! I'm just as twisted and hard and ruthless as you are . . . in my way. I want what I want, and nothing to stop me. And in some ugly black hole deep inside me, I'm glad she's dead! And I hate myself for being glad!"

She commenced crying again and wouldn't let Rady touch her. But as she calmed down she turned to him and clung to him. "I'm scared," she said, "Rady, I'm scared!"

"No need to be," he told her, smoothing her hair and gentling her. "No need to be at all. It's over an' done with now. No need to be feelin' nothin' about it. Annie's gone, an' ever' thing's goin' to be all right."

Annie was killed right after the turn of the year. First week in January, facts is. I recollect it had been unseasonable warm till the day we dug the grave. Then the ground froze under a hard blizzard and we had a heap of trouble with the digging. We never had so much trouble with Mister Rowe's for it was September then, and right after a hard soaking rain at that.

Some was surprised that she wanted him buried in the graveyard on the ridge. Allowed she would of sent him back east where they came from. And she made no explanations. Not even to the sexton when she went over to see about a grave site. Just asked him if she could buy a lot. And when he told her they were all free, she went out and picked one and that's where he was put away. Over in the corner at the far side. The funeral went the queerest of any we'd ever seen on New Ridge. Not no services at the church, with the opening of the casket and folks filing by to take the last look, nor any sermon, nor nothing we were used to at all. Just a gathering at the graveside, and a preacher saying a prayer, and that was all. Junie thought it went plumb heathen. She misdoubted Mister Rowe's soul could get very far towards heaven with such a scant send-off.

"Junie," I says, "hit ain't the kind of funeral a man has gits him to heaven, fur as I've heared tell of. Hit's what he's been an' the way he's lived."

"An' what way is that?" she wanted to know. "Hit just goes to show," she says, "an' it's jist as well she never wanted no preachin', fer what man of God could git up an' truthful say a good word of a man has drunk hisself to death!"

To my mind there's sins a heap worse than drinking, if it's kept under control. A drink or two, or even a fine roistering drunk once in a while don't do nobody any harm. But it was true, and there for all to see, that Mister Rowe had plumb drunk himself into that grave on the far side of the cemetery. It was common knowledge that since early spring he'd been drunk and sick and drunk and sick until that was all he was all the time. Drunk and sick. He never got over one till it ran into another, until time was when you might say he never drew a sober breath. It was a pitying thing to watch. And there was no keeping it from the whole settlement.

He'd come home from Louisville after that sick spell, weak and trembly, and for a time during the winter he was housebound and ill. But it looked like he'd commenced getting better along towards February and March. I saw him out in the yard one day when it was warmer than common for that time of year. He was walking around looking at the snowdrops and first March lilies. He looked a little stouter to me. I stopped a minute to talk and asked him if he was feeling any better. He was white and shaky, but I thought he'd fleshened up a mite.

"A little," he told me, "I think I'm stronger. When it gets warm so I can get out I'll have more strength, perhaps."

I allowed he would too, and passed on.

I saw Rady that same day. He was burning his tobacco beds, and I passed the time of day with him.

He'd been making out by himself since Annie died. Been doing his own cooking and cleaning and getting along as best he could. And as near as I could tell he was making a fair out of it. He could always turn his hand to nearly anything, though, and do good with it. But folks allowed it wouldn't be long till he was casting his eyes around for another woman. A man don't stay a widower long on the ridge. It's too unhandy. I thought to joke him a little about it and asked him if he had anybody in mind yet.

"Shore," he said, laughing hearty, "I got her all picked out."

"Well, now, that's fine," I says. "I dislike to see a old stallion like you goin' to bed by hisself of a night. Git out of the habit first thing you know!"

"I dislike to do it," he says, "an' I'm some afeared of fergittin' how myself. I'm aimin' on takin' steps jist as soon as it's proper."

"Would it discommode you any," I says, "to tell me who you got in mind?"

"It would," he says, "it would discommode me like hell. It ain't none of yore damn business. Besides, you'd tell Junie an' Junie'd tell ever'body on the ridge, an' it would end up me not gittin' to do my own proposin'!"

I couldn't help but laugh, for that's exactly what would of happened, had he already had one picked. People sure do have a habit of gossipin'.

And then I recollected seeing Mister Rowe. "Jist seen Mister Rowe," I told Rady. "He looks some stouter to me than he did."

"Outside, was he?" Rady asked.

"Yeah. He was walkin' around in the yard. Might be if he'd lay off likker fer a time he'd git all right."

"Hit might be," Rady said.

It was getting on in the evening by then and I had to get on back and help do up the work. I said so and got up off the stump I'd been setting on.

"I see," Rady says, grinning, "Junie's still got you henpecked."

It always hackles me for anybody to accuse me of being henpecked. I ain't. But a man'd be a fool not to take the easiest way he can to get along with his woman. Specially if she's strong-minded like Junie. It even hackled me a little with Rady, who had a way of kidding a man could take. "You jist wait," I says to him, more than half-way meaning it, "till you git yore next woman! I hope she's as ill-grained as a dominecker hen! I hope she jist tromps all over you an' keeps yore nose to the grindstone till it's whetted down! I hope she's got a tongue forked like a snake's! An' I hope she slicks the hide offen you with it! I hope she's cross-eyed, buck-toothed an' got a wart on her chin!"

Rady commenced laughing. "My, my," he says, "mebbe I better stay single with all them hopes of yore'n!"

"Jist don't call me henpecked!" I says.

"Why," he says, "you know I think a heap of Junie. Ain't no

better woman on the ridge than Junie. An' smart! She's as bright as a tenpenny nail!"

"An' jist about as unbendin'," I says.

And then we both commenced laughing and I went on home. Something about having a little set-to with Rady always made me feel good. He set as easy with me as a pair of old shoes. Common and comfortable and roomy. You could kid with him, or fight with him, drink with him, hunt with him, fish with him . . . and he fitted smooth and fine. Being with him always made me feel good.

It wasn't much after that, when the weather had faired considerably and we could all stir, that Mister Rowe commenced drinking again. I don't know what Miz Rowe would of done without Rady. For he stayed by, much as he could spare the time from work, and helped with Mister Rowe, nursing him through the crazy, violent times, setting up with him nights when he was the sickest, waiting on him, doing for him. He stayed by right to the last, and was there when he died, in the midst of the craziest spell of all.

I was there that night too, for Mister Rowe had got so bad one man couldn't handle him, and Rady sent for me. He said Miz Rowe oughtn't to see him like that. And he was a sight to see, without any doubts. Thinned down to a skeleton, and pasty white, his eyes sunk deep in his head, and his hands looking like picked bones. It was enough to scare a body the way he'd gone down. We had to hold him on the bed, and he kept screaming and trying to tear loose from us. He kept begging Rady for a drink. As crazy as he was, he was enough in his right mind to keep begging and pleading for a drink.

"Rady!" he'd scream till you could hear him all over the house. "Rady!" And then he'd moan and grab at Rady and beg. "Rady, you've not ever let me down. You're not going to make me do without are you? Just one, Rady. Just a little one. I'd have died, Rady, if it hadn't been for you this summer. You aren't going to let me down now, are you?" Over and over again, but keeping his voice down low except when a pain would hit him and he'd scream

Rady's name. It was like he was whispering something only him and Rady knew.

Finally Rady got up and went to the clothes closet and got a bottle down. He give him a big slug. Mister Rowe got quiet right straight, and Rady stoppered the bottle and instead of putting it back in the closet, he put it in his own hip pocket, kind of absent-minded like. He stood looking down at Mister Rowe, and then he looked at me. "He would of died soon or late anyhow," he said. "I figgered the pore sunovabitch might as well die happy."

It came over me when we'd laid him out later, and were keeping the watch the rest of the night, that I'd been wrong when I'd said one time that Annie couldn't help Rady get old man Hall's place. She'd helped him after all by dying. And it came over me, too, that the brown maid wasn't the only one had a house and land. Fair Elinore had a house and land, too. But for once I kept my mouth shut. I didn't allow this was a time Rady would want to be reminded of either one of them.

It was a funny thing, too, that Miz Rowe never put a headstone for Mister Rowe. She planted a rosebush at the head of his grave instead. Junie was passing the day she planted it and stopped to help her. "Is it a climbin' rose," she asked.

"No" Miz Rowe said, "it's a hybrid. The name of the rose is Peace."

Chapter Fifteen

There were those that allowed Miz Rowe would sell out, now that Mister Rowe was gone, and go back where she'd come from. "What would she stay fer?" they said. "They's nothin' to keep her here on New Ridge now."

And when she lit out a couple of weeks after the funeral they nodded their heads together and said the next thing would be a sale of the property, and there was a heap of figuring what it would bring and who would get it. Most figured Rady would bid it in.

But I never allowed that was the way he'd get it. And I figured, not that I ever named it, even to Junie, that there was a heap to keep Miz Rowe on the ridge, and I allowed she'd be coming back in a decent and respectful time.

Facts is, if she'd had her way she wouldn't of never left. That was Rady's idea, not hers. "I don't want to go," she said to him. "Why should I go away and spend the winter?"

"Hit'll look better," he told her.

"I don't care how it looks!"

"I do. Besides, it'd be hard on you stayin' here by yerself through the cold."

"There's no place to go."

"Yer folks?"

"I don't have any folks."

"His folks, then."

"No! I hate that old man!"

"All right, then, go to Florida. Like you used to do."

"And what would I use for money?"

"They's money."

"Yours?"

"What difference does it make? It's mine or yours, mine an' yours, jist dependin' on which way you look at it. It kin be spared, anyways."

"How do you know I'd come back?"

He grinned at her. "Well, I don't, to say, know it. But I figger you would. Is they somethin' you'd ruther do?"

It was chilly for the last of September and the windows were closed and a little fire was burning on the hearth. Miz Rowe held her hands out close to the fire like they had got cold of sudden. "No," she said finally. "But I wish there was!"

"You're jist nervous an' upset," Rady told her. "Go ahead an' take the winter somewheres, an' then come back next spring. We'll git married along in the summer."

She walked over to the window and pressed her forehead against the glass and looked out. The leaves were already turning on the trees and the grass in the yard was bleaching. A few late flowers were still in bloom, but a gust of wind blew along the vines, and some petals shook down and fell. "I don't know whether I want to marry you or not," she said.

"Why?"

"It would be a damn fool thing to do."

Rady had been setting by the fire, but he stood up then and walked over to the door. He stopped there with his hand on the knob. "That's jist up to you," he said. "You want to sell me this place an' git shut of it an' me at the same time?"

When he'd stood up she'd turned to look at him, and she watched him now, his hand on the doorknob, ready to go. And it was like she knew he could and would walk right through the door and never look back. Could walk right out of her life and forget her and put behind him what had been between them.

Could do without it, and without her, and no bother to him. It must be a terrible thing for a woman to have that kind of knowing inside her, and to know at the same time, because of her own weakness, there's not a thing she can do about it. It must be pure galling. It was no wonder she stood there with her hands made into fists and her face white and the tears running down her cheeks and saying to him, "I could kill you! And I hate you, Rady Cromwell! I hate you!"

Standing there looking at him with hate and madness. And then, when he turned his back on her and commenced opening the door, breaking, and running to snatch at him to feel him safe and solid and big and still there, not going and not forgetting. She flung herself at him, and when he closed his arms around her, she laid her head against his chest and cried. "And I love you, I love you! And I can't live without you!"

So she went away for a time, I don't remember exactly how long it was. Several months, though. And then she came back, and Rady commenced courting her proper. There was talk, of course. But it went natural. It was the kind of talk went the rounds when any man commenced courting a woman. Just a kind of curious gossip. "Seen Rady an' Miz Rowe over at the county fair yesterday. Reckon they'll be gittin' hitched one of these days."

"Likely."

And if it was a man doing the talking he'd grin and add, "I shore would like to be in Rady Cromwell's shoes! He's the luckiest guy ever I seen!"

Wasn't never no putting things together nor trying to add things up the way it had come about both him and her were free. There was just a watching and talking and nodding of heads, and mostly a wondering when they'd get married.

It was in August when they went over to the county seat and had old Judge Morgan marry them. Didn't nobody go with them, for they hadn't named their intentions to a soul. They just went over and got their license and went to the judge's office. He called in a couple of witnesses from the hallway and it was done in five minutes' time. I did hear that when they'd left, the judge spit hard into his old brass spittoon and looked over his spectacles at one of the witnesses and said, "That boy shore likes widders, don't he?"

So Rady moved again. Him and his dog and his gittar and his gun. And he now was the owner of the best farm in the settlement, living in the best house on the ridge, and married to the handsomest woman. He had it all now. The fields, stretching wide and far. The timbered woods. The barns and the herds and the fine, good farm tools. He could saddle up Mister Rowe's horse and ride half a day to bound his land, for with the two places lying side by side and thrown together he had more than a quarter of all the level land on top the ridge. All of the best. That was what he had now.

And he lived in the big, fine house, with the electric all over and water in the kitchen. With the books and the guns and the big piano. With the shiny furniture and the shiny floors. With the fine dishes, and the thin glasses and the solid silver. And he hung his clothes in the bedroom closet, and he slept with Miz Rowe in the tall, four-poster bed. And there wasn't a sign of a ghost to haunt either his mounting or his sleeping.

"Don't you never," I asked him once, "think about Mister Rowe dyin' in that very same bed?"

"Naw," he said, grinning. "Why would I?"

"I dunno. I'd ruther have me a brand-splinter new bed, if it was me."

"Hit suits me fine," he said. "I've allus admired that bed. Why would I buck agin the bed? Ever'thing else come from him too. From the land plumb down to the woman."

I could only shake my head. I'd still of rather had me a new bed, had it been me.

It was that same day Rady named a proposition to me.

"Whyn't you an' Junie," he says, "move over to Annie's house?"

"I ain't got no reason to move over to Annie's house," I said.

"You would have if you run my new sawmill fer me," he said.

It was the first I'd heard of a sawmill. "You aimin' on startin' you up a mill?"

He nodded. "Got me a good engine over at town the other day. I was thinkin' I'd commence cuttin' in them woods that joins the two places. Heap of good trees in there needs cuttin'. An' I'd ruther do it than to turn a crew loose in there to slash out the young stuff the way they do."

"Heap ruther make all the money yerself, too, hadn't you?"

He laughed. "Well, I got too much good timber now to go dividin' the profits up amongst too many."

I had nothing to lose by moving over to Annie's place. Wasn't as if I was selling out. I could keep my own place till I needed it again, and live better at Annie's, it being a sight better house. Junie liked the idea, too, except she never was very crazy about me working for Rady. But he was the only man I'd of worked a day for, me liking to be my own boss the way I do. And it would be a good way of making cash money all through the winter.

So that's the way me and Junie happened to move to Annie's house, and the way me and Rady commenced, you might say, working together. I had in mind to work the winter and then go back to my own place and make my crop. But again the winter was over we had Rady's timber cut and he'd got out and contracted for a heap more. "Stay on," he said to me. "You'll make more on wages with me then you would to raise a crop this year." And I allowed he was right, so I stayed on.

When spring came he had his hands full with the farm, so he got Duke Simmons to help me at the mill. Duke was a good hand, but the logs kept rolling in till it was more than the two of us could handle. So it wasn't long till I had to tell Rady I'd have to have another hand. He sent the oldest Pringle boy down to help. "How come you kin spare Eddie from the farm?" I asked him.

"Flary's come home to stay," he said. "She'll take his place in the field."

I couldn't help but grin. "I don't reckon you had ary thing to do with her comin' back," I said.

Rady grinned too. "I never had nothin' to do with it," he said. "'Course, it might of been that the rumor Flary was carryin' on with the woman's husband right under her nose influenced her some in gettin' shut of her."

"Was she?"

"Hell, I don't know. But I wanted the girl closer home."

"You been rollin' her right along?"

"Some . . . of late. She's pretty good."

Things rocked along. Miz Rowe neighbored with Junie as much as it was in her nature to neighbor, I reckon. She'd come over several times a month to set and talk, and seem like she got real fond of the young'uns. She had a sewing machine and she was real handy with it and she was always running up a dress for Junie or some shirts for the boys. Junie kind of unthawed towards her, gradual, and finally allowed that since she'd married Rady she was right nice. "She ain't near so stuck-up an' high-an'-mighty," she said. "She ast fer my corn ketchup recipe the other day. Said she'd heared I made the best in the settlement."

As best she could Miz Rowe settled into the ways of the ridge. But a noticing person could of told by the end of the first year they were married, she wasn't very happy deep down inside. She wasn't cut out to be a ridge runner. Sometimes I think you got to be born here amongst these hills to love them, and the ways of the people have got to be your ways, bred into you from way back, before you can understand them. You got to know you come from a long line of folks that always had to be pushing ahead of the towns to places where they weren't hemmed in and smothered, before you can know the feeling was a need in them and is still a need in you. New Ridge is a dark and lonesome place, and the hollers are deep and quiet. But if you were born here, there's no other place in the world where you can feel at home and be content. The people are strange and queer, with their own ideas of right and wrong, and good and bad, unless they're your own people, and it may be then you're strange and queer along with them. I don't know how an outsider could get to know and love the ridge ways, unless he could put behind him everything he'd ever known different, and forget there was anything more than the ridge in the world.

Miz Rowe couldn't do that. She'd been used to too much, and she couldn't never forget it. She brought it with her to the ridge, and it set her apart. Mister Rowe had been different along with her, and they made a kind of world of their own together. But she was married to a ridge man now, and she might as well of butted her head against a stone wall as to set herself to change him or his ways. There wasn't nothing for her to do but wear the harness where it galled the most. And it was the little things where it galled.

Like sleeping with Rady. It wasn't the crazy, wild, hungry feeding of themselves any more. It was there now, casual, regular, still good but only middling good . . . lawfully good . . . and not very high-blazing. And after, there was the sleep. Rady snoring and thrashing the bed, being a restless sleeper like he was. Eight, nine, ten hours of sleep. Rady's always laid down soon, and being wore out with the long days at the mill and on the farm, he'd want to get to bed by good dark. "My God!" she said, frashed beyond keeping quiet one night, "it's only eight o'clock! Can't you stay awake one night? Can't you talk? Do you have to sit there and nod and snore and drool? Turn the radio on, or read, or say something! You're just an animal! Working and sleeping and eating!"

Rady got up and commenced taking his clothes off. "I'm tired an' I'm sleepy, an' I'm goin' to bed. You kin turn the radio on if you want, or read, or set here an' talk to yerself. I like to sleep when I'm sleepy."

When she followed him into the bedroom she looked at his overhalls hanging on the post of the bed with disgust. She'd always seen him in overhalls. But seeing them hang on the post of her bed was something different. Rady was clean for a ridge man, cleaner than most. But you can't farm and work a mill without getting dirty, and dirt that close to her was something Miz Rowe had never seen before. She couldn't stand his overhalls and denim shirts and heavy work shoes. And she had to stand them right next to her.

And there were three meals a day to cook for him, which Rady always relished. Sometimes she'd set and look at him eating, the same way all us ridge folks eat, elbows sprawled out over the table, shoveling the food in fast, chewing three or four times and swallowing it down with a gulp. "You eat like a hog!" she told him once.

Rady never even paused or looked up. "You kin wait an' eat by yerself," he told her, "you don't like the way I eat. Hit's food, ain't it? Whichever way you git it down."

And times, the way he talked made her put her hands over

her ears. She never said so, but it must of crossed her mind many a time that she'd drove her ducks to a bad market. Mister Rowe had been a drunkard, but he'd been a gentleman drunkard. He could stay up till a respectable bedtime without nodding in his chair. He could talk, and did so, about anything . . . books, music, the world and the times. And he could play his piano hours on end, making his own inside world come to light and shine. He'd had the polish and the ease that money and travel and breedin' give a man . . . and that even in his cups he never quite forgets. He'd had the same things she'd had all her life. Liked the same things she'd liked. Their ways had been the same, their talk, their knowledge and their understanding. When she'd set a little table on the brick paving out under the mulberry tree, set it with thin linen and fine china and bring silver, Mister Rowe had known what she meant and had liked it with her. When she set the same table for Rady, it never meant any more than if she'd put crockery on an oilcloth in the kitchen for him. Mister Rowe had liked breaded shrimp, and green, herb-flavored salads, and old cheese and crisp crackers. Rady liked soup beans and corn bread and turnip greens. He wanted a square meal under his belt. He had no patience with her finickyness, and he let her see it. She had no patience with his ridge ways, and she let him see that.

Still, they made out. It wasn't no worse marriage than many, and better than some. Miz Rowe was too much of a lady to do more than nag a little, and it never mattered a lot to Rady. He got just what he wanted out of the marriage. He hadn't expected things to stay the same between them. He'd known what being married would do to that high-blowing flame. He'd known when he married her that he'd already had the best. He didn't know or care that marriage could be different. You married, and then you had you a woman to do for you. Some women were stout and able and easy-going, like Annie had been. Some were nervous and twitchy and cross-grained, like Miz Rowe. It made precious little difference in the way of your days. It made handier to have a woman than not, but the land and the tobacco and the corn, and the herd of beef cattle and the sawmill . . . those were the important things. They were what counted.

He'd liked the free-giving, free-loving ways of Annie and he
had taken them, but he'd liked her farm better. He'd liked the
hard-tempered blade of Miz Rowe's bending, and he'd used it, but
he liked her farm better. Like he wouldn't of cared had Annie been
as old and haggy as his own grandma, he wouldn't of cared had
Miz Rowe been as spindly and spent-flamed as a guttering candle.
The important thing about each woman had been what she'd owned
and brought in solid value to Rady when she married him.

He counted it pure good luck that both women had been
good in bed. What he never did see was that if they hadn't of been
good in bed, he might never of got either one of them. He counted
on it and used it for a net with both of them. But he never saw
that his net would of been full of holes hadn't they both been of
the nature to want and need a strong mating. And both been
starved for it.

But Miz Rowe wasn't starved no longer, and one day when
Junie was over there she got her to help her take down the big
four-poster bed and move it in the back room. And she moved two
narrow beds in hers and Rady's room. "Said Rady tumbled around
so in bed she couldn't sleep," Junie told me. "Hit might be a good
idee at that," she went on, "hit would bear thinkin' on. If I could
git you in another bed, mebbe I'd skip a couple of years havin' a
young'un!"

"I'd jist like to see you try it!" I told her.

And she giggled. For all her fussing I allowed it pleased her
for me to set my foot down. I never held with such foolishness.
The place for a man and woman that's married is together. They
might sleep better apart, but they'd lose more than they'd gain.
For there isn't anything better in being married than the plain
and simple act of sharing a bed. Outside the loving, it's the knowing the other one is there. To lie in the dark and talk to, maybe.
To snuggle to and get warm. To roll against in the night and feel
good because they're there to touch. Junie's slept with one or the
other of the young'uns when they were ailing, but it was always
a lonesome time for me. I wasn't about to have her getting in
such an idea of making it lasting!

I don't reckon it made any difference to Rady one way or the other. I allow he paid her a visit when he wanted to, and as often as he wanted. And there was always Flary if Miz Rowe wasn't in the notion, or if she was, for that matter. That part of his life was the least of his worries those days.

They were sure fine, fat times. And Rady was making them count big. Looked like everything he turned his hand to turned out good for him. The seasons were right for two years hand-running, and he made big crops and got a high market on them. His hogs and beef weighed heavy and brought good prices, and he kept buying and buying. And he kept so far out ahead on contracts at the mill that I didn't know as we'd ever get caught up and didn't care. Rady was making money hand over fist, and I was making more along with him than I'd ever thought to make.

Rady never had no time nor thought to spare for nothing but work. Miz Rowe or Flary, he took them both when he wanted and it was handy, and one meant about as much to him as the other. He was riding a high tide, and he was as sure as sin it would keep on rising. He made bigger and bigger plans all the time, and he kept every dime he could get hold of tied up in more stock, and more pastures, and more tools and more timber to saw. And he loved every minute of it. To get, and keep on getting. Seeing no end to it. That was the way he came up to the winter of 1929. Walking big, riding high, straddling the world.

They'd been married a little better than three years that fall, and Miz Rowe got in the family way. It was their first one, and not being ridge born, she talked about it right straight to Junie, and commenced making big plans for it. She bought up a lot of goods and sewed it into the littlest dresses ever I saw, and bought a thing she called a bass-i-net and lined it with pink silk. She got a little bathtub and painted it and put pictures of babies and animals all over it, and she even came home from town one day with a toy rabbit, all white and woolly, with shoe-button eyes! Junie told her it was bad luck to commence making plans so soon, but she just laughed at her and went right on. I'd not ever seen her as happy as she was those days. She was dead sure it was going to be a little girl. It did go the queerest to hear her talking right out about having a baby, and showing baby clothes and toys and things. Junie thought it was downright indecent, but I kind of liked it myself. Seemed like she was having a lot of fun anyways.

Rady never had much time to pay her any attention, although he appeared glad enough about the baby. He joked with her some about it, and just to see her get her dander up would say he'd throw a little old girl in the creek . . . he was aiming to have a boy. But funny things had commenced to happen on the market. He wasn't, to say, worried when his hogs and beef brought a lot lower price, and he wasn't too uneasy when the market on lumber fell off. "Hit'll pick up," he said, "jist keep on sawin'." And he went on buying.

We sawed till we had a yard full. We were sawing a heap faster than it was moving, and it kept on stacking up till there wasn't hardly any place to put it. Still Rady kept on making contracts, paying out his money for timber and not being able to move the lumber when it was sawed.

"Rady, you better pull in," I told him, "you better take what you kin git fer what's on hand, an' go easy on new contracts."

"An' lose money?" he said. "Hit'll pick up agin. Naw, I ain't sellin' on this market. We'll hold it till it goes up agin."

And on a low market he kept buying more and more stock, till he was having to buy feed, not having raised enough, even with all the land he'd turned into corn and pastures. It made me plumb uneasy, but it was like he had a fever to keep on getting more stuff. "Now's the time to buy," he said, "while stuff's cheap. Sell high, later."

"An' supposin' you have to sell cheaper?" I said.

"I won't. Hit'll pick up. Next year you'll see. I'll make so much money I won't never have to do another lick of work!"

But I was still uneasy. There was talk of it lasting, this low market. Talk of a stock market crash and things going crazy outside. Talk of things getting awful tight. I wouldn't of wanted everything I had tied up in something I had to sell. I would of rather had it in cash money myself. I was glad I had a little stashed away. Worst came to worst, it'd run us till I could get a crop made. But as long as Rady sawed, I'd run the mill, I reckoned.

Chapter Sixteen

In banking they've got a term I never knew much about, but I saw what it meant that spring. Rady was over-extended. He owed for timber he'd made contracts for, and he owed for stock he'd bought. And he had to count on the stock paying for both. He might have made it, and I don't say he wouldn't, if a thing hadn't happened and turned the wheel in the wrong direction, and it came from a quarter he least suspected of ever giving him a minute's trouble.

Miz Rowe was getting on towards six months, going around in kind of a glow, not knowing or caring that Rady was up to his ears in worries. Being kind of little and scant-weighted most times, she showed a heap, like Junie's orange in the middle of a stocking. And it was getting harder for her to do up her work. She hadn't been none too stout all along, the doctor warning her to keep her from having bad luck. Junie said she never had seen a woman have the morning sickness so bad. And when that was past there was something else made her ankles and legs swell sometimes. But she'd taken care all along, and she was still taking care.

She spoke to Junie one day about getting somebody to come in and help. Junie would of gone and glad to, could she have spared the time. But she always had her hands full. "Whyn't you git Flary?" she said, trying to think of somebody close. "Looks like they could spare her fer a couple or three months."

Miz Rowe knew, of course, that Flary was at home, and knew she was making a hand along with the old man and the boys. She'd seen her a time or two the first year she was home, but not of late. "Why, I hadn't thought of her," she said. "Can she do housework?"

"Well, she was hired out to some woman over in town. I reckon she kin make out, though I wouldn't say how good she'd be. Leastways, she could do the heavy work fer you."

"I'll go over there right now and talk to her," Miz Rowe said.

"You better see what Rady says first, hadn't you?" Junie said. "See if he kin spare her."

"It doesn't matter whether he can spare her or not," Miz Rowe said, kind of sniffing. "He can get somebody else for the field. Help's too scarce for me to pass up somebody right at my door!" And she lit out to have a talk with Flary.

Had Junie known what I knew she would of died before she breathed Flary's name. But she never, and Miz Rowe ran right smack into it.

She went over to the Pringles and made her way through the litter in the front yard. The old woman came to the door. "Is Flary home?" Miz Rowe asked her.

In a way it was like the old woman was glad to see her. She grinned. "She shore is," she said. "Come in. She's on the bed. She ain't been feelin' so good lately."

And Miz Rowe went in. Flary got up off the bed. I don't reckon anything could of hit more sudden and unexpected. Flary's dress was hiking up in front just as much as Miz Rowe's, if not a little more. She stood there and looked at Miz Rowe. And Miz Rowe stood and looked at her. Both bulged and out of shape, and both got that way by the same man. Miz Rowe just stood and looked and never said a word. Then she commenced laughing and she turned around and walked out of the house, never once looking back nor even faltering. Just walked off, turning her back on Rady's bastard big in Flary, and carrying her own bigness awkwardly with her. She knew. There wasn't a doubt in her mind.

When she got home she went straight to the barn and saddled her horse, and ungainly as she was, she got on him and headed like the wind for the road. She'd not been riding since she'd known about the baby. She'd been taking good care. But it was like she wanted a purpose now to ride the devil away, or to rid herself of something unclean and unwanted. It was like she went a little crazy, and wanted, maybe, to join Annie and her young'un over in the graveyard. Like they'd had the best of it, after all. Leastways that's what I always made of it.

And she came close to it. Junie saw her pounding down the road and she came tearing over the mill to get me. "Miz Rowe's gone plumb out of her head," she said. "She's on that horse agin, an' she went past our place goin' like the wind. She'll lose that young'un, shore!"

I lit out down the road, Junie keeping up behind as best she could. But it was more than a couple of miles before we came up to her. The horse was cropping grass by the side of the road and Miz Rowe was setting in the saddle, her face white, her hands gripping the pommel and all bent over. It was easy to tell the jolting and pounding had started things.

"Have you done an' lost yer mind?" Junie scolded when we came up. "Haven't you got a grain of sense left in yer head!"

She looked at Junie and her eyes had a kind of dull look. "I don't care," she says, and then she kind of moaned and hung onto the pommel of the saddle again. "I don't care! I don't want it! I hate it! I hate it! Let it die. It ought to die! Let him have Flary's!" And she shuddered. "Maybe we'll both die."

"She's out of her head," Junie said, but I knew about what had happened. I told Junie. And she looked at me with her eyes as big as wheels. "My God," she said, "hit was me sent her over there!"

We got her down off the horse and Junie made her lie down on the grass and then she sent me for Rady. He'd bought a car the year before and could get there quick. He came as fast as he could, scared to death and as white as a sheet himself. I told him, best I could, what had happened. I wouldn't of wanted to be in his shoes. I don't know as I could of faced it. But he did. But like many another man before him, he took out his feelings by being short with her. "What in hell's the matter with you?" he said, gruff and mad. "Ain't you got no sense?"

She never said a word to him. Hardly looked at him, and when he touched her to lift her in the car, she pulled away from him, like his hands were dirty and filthy.

She lost the baby. And it was a little girl. But she never acted like she cared one way or the other. She never asked about it, or seemed to grieve. She just laid there sick and white, not talking to anybody. The only time she ever showed any life was when Rady would try to come in the room. She made them keep him out. She could storm and scream at him hard enough, and she wouldn't have him anywheres close. "Keep him out of here," she'd yell, and if he'd come in anyhow, she'd throw anything she could lay her hands on at him, cursing him and squalling and screaming. He didn't try but once or twice to see her. After that he went his way and left her to herself.

She was a time getting over it. A month or two, as I remember. She was up and around sooner, but not stout by any means. Junie went when she could and helped, but things got in a right smart mess, and it was mostly Rady had to redd up himself. Miz Rowe never cared. Just walked through the clutter and around it like it wasn't there. And I misdoubt she said a dozen words to Rady all that time. It was like he wasn't there, either.

Then she seemed to make up her mind of a sudden about things. He came home one evening and she was packing her clothes. "What you doin'?" he asked her.

"I'm leavin'," she said.

"Leavin'?"

She had her bags laid out on the bed and was folding things neat like her old way of doing. But she turned around to look at him. "I'm leaving the whole goddamned mess. You and the ridge and Flary Pringle and everything else! I'm leaving it! All of it!"

It took the wind out of Rady and he set down all at once. "Fer good?" he says.

"God, yes, for good! Forever and ever good!"

"You aimin' on gittin' a divorce?"

"Just as soon as I can!"

A hundred things must of run through his head, quick and flashing. The place was hers. She'd heired it from Mister Rowe, and she'd never had a joint deed made. It was hers, out and out. Rady'd never thought about trouble with her, and he'd never worried about the deed. What a woman owned, her man owned with her. But here it was. And Rady had to have the place if he was going to get out of the jam he'd got himself in. He'd be ruined if he lost it. And if she got a divorce . . . well, he figured he'd lost it.

He pulled himself up out of the chair and went over to her. He tried to put his arms around her. "Cordy . . ." he said, trying to hold onto her and turn her so's he could talk to her. "Cordy . . ."

But if he meant to say he was sorry, if he meant to try to hold her with what had once held her, it was too late. It was too much water over the dam, and it was all gone. With all the strength she had she twisted loose from him and slapped him across the face so hard he rocked back on his heels. "So help me, I'll kill you if you try to touch me again," she hissed at him.

Looking at her he had the notion she looked a heap like she did the first time he ever saw her, her face carved and white and still and her eyes full of hate and fury, the pupils widening with her hate. Even her hair hung like it did then, black and soft like a little girl's, around her face. There was no misdoubting her. She was through and Rady knew it. So he turned around and walked out of the room and out of the house and off the place. He never saw her again.

Chapter Seventeen

That was the begining of the end. Miz Rowe left and in time got her divorce. But even before she got the divorce she had the law on Rady and had him put off the place. It was her way of striking back. And it was a good way. He lost his hay and his corn and a good part of his stock. It forced his hand and he had to commence selling.

He sold the lumber first, but what he got for it didn't even pay out the contracts. For the contracts had been made high, and he had to sell mighty low. Then he sold the mill, for less than half what he'd paid for the whole set-up. But it was clear and he paid off his contracts with that money. Not a dime, though, did he have left over.

She put the place up for sale and Rady tried to buy it. With no money he went to the bank and slapped a mortgage on Annie's place and tried to bid it in. But the bank wouldn't let him have enough to handle the deal and he had to see it go to a stranger. Fellow from over on the pike.

Me and Junie moved back to our place, and Rady moved over to Annie's house again. He oughtn't to of kept the mortgage money when he couldn't buy in Miz Rowe's place, of course. But he was about crazy trying to save what he could of his stock. He had too many to run on Annie's place, so he had to sell some, and he never got back his buying price for them, and still owed plenty. So he hung onto the money to try to feed them and run what he had until he could get a better price.

He put in a big crop of corn and more tobacco than common that spring. He worked day and night like a man devil-chased, pulling out of this corner only to get into that one. But he never gave up. He never quit trying. Like a bulldog hanging on, he kept trying. He sweated and he cussed and he got as thin as a rail and as tough as shoe leather. I got real uneasy about him. "Rady," I said to him one day, "you're killin' yer fool self. The world'll still turn if you lose ever'thing you got, but if you ain't here to see it, it shore won't do you no good fer it to be turnin'."

He just shook his head. "I'll be here," he said, "an' I'll lick it. I'm goin' to seed me another pasture come fall, an' I'll git me ten more head of stock."

There wasn't no use arguing with him. He was the way he was. He had to keep trying. Me, I wasn't in no danger of losing my place, but we'd had to pull in our belts a right smart. I had to lay out most of our cash to get us through until market time. But everybody was having a rough time as far as I could see. And we weren't the only ones had mush and milk for supper, I reckon. But we had a roof over our heads, and there was always something to eat, and the fish never quit biting. I allow it'd pass in time, and there was no use frashing myself about it.

I disremember the exact time, but I know it was early in the summer that Flary had her young'un. The Pringles had moved back down to old man Crewel's and glad to get there. Flary had gone with them, naturally. I recollect I had stopped by Rady's to borrow the use of his grindstone. My scythe had gone dull on me. "Use it an' welcome," he said. "I'll pour fer you."

He straddled the horse and commenced pedaling, pouring the water at the same time in a steady, slow trickle. I laid the blade against the stone. Putting an edge on a blade is a thing requires care and concentration. The stone has got to turn just so. The water has got to trickle just right. And the man handling the blade has got to take care what he's doing. We got a perfect edge on that scythe, and then we set down in the shade and talked awhile. Rady had commenced chewing instead of smoking so much. Cheaper, I reckon. And he had a plug of Old Mule would of bit the tongue off the original mule!

"Reckon you've heared," he said after a while, "Flary's had her kid."

"No," I says, "when?"

"Last week."

"You seen it?"

He nodded. "Hit's a boy." And then he grinned from ear to ear. "Dammed if the little sunovabitch don't look exactly like Pa!"

I like to of swallowed my plug!

When I told Junie she kind of snorted. "Hit jist goes to show," she said, "the truth'll stand when the world's on fire!"

Just what truth she had in mind wasn't very clear to me.

That fall corn dropped to three cents and tobacco went to seven. Nobody had ever heard of such prices! You couldn't even make your haul bill to market! It was the bottom dropped out! It was the end of everything known and counted on. A man didn't know what to do or where to turn. Everybody was scared and uneasy. Nobody had any idea of how to make out, except just to keep on the best way he could.

Except Rady. He came over one day right after dinner. "Git yer gun," he says, "let's see if we kin skeer up a squirrel or two."

Even the squirrels were scarcer than hen's teeth. Looked like they knew it was a bad time for any of them to show, folks needing stuff to eat like they did. We didn't get any squirrels, but we didn't, to say, do much squirrel hunting. When we got over in the holler Rady laid his gun up beside a tree and set down. "Listen," he says, "I'm goin' to lose my place an' ever'thing I got if I don't do somethin' an' do it quick. I can't even pay the interest on that mortgage, an' you know they ain't goin' to wait long on me."

"Rady, I ain't got a dime . . ." I was commencing to say.

But he cut me short. "I ain't tryin' to borry. Look, I ain't sellin' my corn fer no three cents. I got a better idee what to do with it. Want to come in with me?"

I didn't like the idea of selling my corn for three cents, either, and I had six young'uns now to feed. "Reckon we could make anything?"

"More'n we kin make sellin' on the market. I already talked to Duke an' he's willin'. An' he's got some sheet copper we kin make a drum out of, an' he knows where he kin git some copper tubin'. We all got corn, an' I reckon between us we kin rake up enough cash to buy the first batch of sugar. You willin'?"

I figured a minute. It was chancey, no doubts, but not too much. Folks around the ridge always did allow it was a man's business what he did with his corn, or his time. Wouldn't be but little chance of getting caught, I figured. Worst was I'd have to keep it from Junie, but maybe she'd think I was fishing and hunting a heap.

"I'm willin'," I told him, then.

So we built us a still over on Little Lost Creek. Good place for it. Backed up against a hill on a little arm of land, and with plenty of good creek water handy. Rady made the drum, and we got some copper tubing for the worm. Never took long, and inside of a couple of weeks we'd run off our first batch. Making moonshine is pretty simple, actually. Anybody could do it. You make up a mash with corn meal, fresh ground is better, and sugar. Scald it and add your creek water and leave it alone till it ferments. Then you get beer, and you dip it into the cooker, put your cap on and commence distilling. You don't want to have too hot a fire or you'll scorch your beer. When you draw it off you got likker. Some guys sell the singlings, but we never. We always run ours through twice, and if I do say so myself, we made a powerfully good moonshine.

And there never was times yet so hard that men couldn't find the money to buy a jug of likker. We did good, right from the start. And it felt fine to have a little cash jingling in our pockets again. We ran off a batch every week, and sold it as fast as we made it. Our county being dry we never had to worry about federal men. It was the county men we had to watch, and we knew most of them.

I got me a new span of mules and got Junie another cow. Duke, who hadn't never married, bought himself a second-hand car. Rady paid off the interest on his mortgage and figured he could hold onto the rest of his stock another year. Flary littered again, with twins, and Rady moved her out of her pa's house into a little cabin down in the holler. Wasn't much of a place. Just an old log shack, one of the first built in the settlement, and it looked about ready to cave in. But it was handy to him. He knew in reason he wasn't the only one visited the cabin. Of a Saturday night used to be a right smart gathering down there. But I reckon Rady always had first call.

We did fine for about a year. But just when you least expect it in things like that, there's a slip sometimes, and the slip came for us when an ornery, low-lifed deputy decided to get smart. It was election year, and he was up for sheriff and wanted to make a showing. He pulled a fast raid on us late one evening. Him and three more men. Caught all three of us at the still. We heard them, and scattered, but there was a gunfight. All three of us were hid behind the rocks on the hillside back of the still, and all three of us were shooting. Which of us killed the deputy I don't to this day know. Could of been any of us. But one thing is sure, one of us did. I saw him drop. But with me and Rady and Duke all firing, and firing fast, there was no way of knowing who got him.

They caught Duke and me, but Rady got away. They took us into the jail, and all I could think about was Junie and the young'uns. She'd be worried to death, I knew. I got the jailer to promise to mail her a letter and I set down and wrote her. Wasn't any use me telling her I was sorry. It was too late for that, and besides I wasn't sorry for nothing but getting caught and having to leave her by herself. I knew we were up for a stiff rap, on account of the deputy being killed. But I knew, too, they couldn't prove it on either one of us, and the most we could get would be manslaughter. That was enough, though. I was glad there was a little money to help Junie out while I was gone.

I hadn't much more than got my letter wrote when the door clanged open and they brought Rady in. You could of knocked me over with a feather! "How'd they find you?" I said.

He set down on the bunk and rolled himself a cigarette. "Didn't," he said. "I give myself up."

"You damned fool!' I yelled at him, "what'd you want to do that fer? You had it made!"

He kind of grinned. "I didn't want you boys to have no fun I wasn't in on."

How do you like that? The gall of the guy! The nerve, the guts! He got away clean and he knew neither Duke nor me would talk. He didn't have to come in and give himself up. He could of stayed clear. They'd of settled for me and Duke. They didn't have nothing on Rady. He was as clean as a blowed nose. But, man, it made me feel fine! Old Rady wasn't going to let us take the rap by ourselves. He was in on it and he was going the whole trip. And he went. A little further than we did.

Because he was trying to get us off cheap, he told that the still was his and said we just worked for him. It didn't hold water, for we weren't having it that way, but he did have more in it than we did, and that came out at the trial, and made him what they called the responsible party. He got twenty years. Me and Duke each got ten.

I served two years and nine months and then got paroled. It was the longest two years and nine months of my life! You got to do time behind bars to know what it's like. There's no way I could tell you. But to a man used to roaming free, used to being his own master, used to space and high skies and woods and creeks and fields and pastures, it's pure hell. It's like a wild animal being caged, and you get so crazy sometimes just to walk beyond walls and gates and people that you feel like you can't stand it another minute. I know why guys go berserk and kill to get out. I felt like it myself more than once. I was sure glad to get out of that place!

Junie was waiting at the gate when I got out. And of course she peeled the hide off my back first thing. But Jesus Christ, I didn't even care! It felt so good to be hearing her laying me out I could of listened to her all day! Right in the middle she got her tongue all tangled up though, and commenced crying, and then she kind of fell all over me, hugging and kissing and crying all mixed up together. "Hush up, Junie," I says, "we're wastin' time! You know how long I been doin' without? A even thousand nights! Let's git on home an' commence makin' another young'un!"

That made her haul up and stick her nose in the air. "Makin' young'uns! Makin' moonshine! Makin' trouble! That's all a man's good fer! You're comin' home with me an' commence makin' a crop, that's what you're goin' to make!"

And right then I never even minded the idea! A tobacco crop sounded plumb nice to me!

Duke got out a couple of months after I did, but Rady had to do six years. Six long, long years. I used to think of him up there, knowing how those walls shut him in and kept the sun and the sky and the sight of hills out. Knowing he was eating his heart out like I'd done, and marking off the days on the calendar in his cell. Knowing how slow the days went and how they were all alike, gray and tedious and endless. But he was a good prisoner, and he got every day coming to him for good behavior. He didn't want to stay any longer than he had to, and the quickest way to get out was to behave himself.

I wrote to him all along. Told him the news. One piece of news I sure hated to have to tell him. The bank took over his place and Jubal Moore bought it in. Same Jubal Moore whose mule we'd stampeded that night at the tent meeting. But you couldn't hold it against him. The place was selling, and it went for a little of nothing. It was smart to buy it in. I wished I'd of had the money to get it for Rady.

He hadn't anything left to come back to now. Not a thing. And when he'd get out all he'd have was ten dollars and a suit of new clothes. Not even any place to go to, except mine and Junie's. His old man had disowned him long ago. As if he had anything to disown with!

Along about the time he was due to get out I wrote him and told him me and Junie would be looking for him. And late one evening he came walking up. I saw him plumb down the road and went to meet him. Same old Rady. Same old grin. Same old rusty hair bushing up. Same spraddling walk. Same shoulders busting out his coat. He didn't even look much older. Man, I was glad to see him! Ever'body was glad to see him. Being penitentiaryed don't amount to nothing around here.

"What you aimin' on doin', Rady?" they says.

"Why, I'm aimin' to farm," he says back to them. "What you think I'm aimin' to do?"

"Allowed mebbe you'd go back to stillin'," they'd say, kind of joking.

"Think I'll stick to farmin'," he says, laughing with them, "the law's gittin' too smart fer a country boy like me."

He took a few days to look around and then he came in one morning and said he was moving out. "Where to?" I asked him.

He grinned at me. "Over at Annie's place. I'm rentin'."

I kind of hated to see him go back over there, but he never seemed to mind. Acted real cheerful about it. I followed him out to the road when he was leaving. "Let me know if they's anything I kin do," I told him.

He said he would, and then like he'd just thought of it he asked, "You know where Flary an' the kids is at?"

"With her folks last I heared," I told him. "They moved out of the holler several years ago."

"She ain't took up with nobody else?"

"Well," I says, "you know Flary. But she ain't livin' with nobody regular, fur as I know."

"Much obleeged," he says, and he turned and commenced walking down the road.

"Rady," I called after him, and he stopped. "They's a couple more kids."

He grinned. "Reckon they can't be laid to me. I ain't good enough to breed long distance."

Then he raised the dust behind him round the bend. So it never surprised me much when Junie came busting in mad as a wet hen a day or two later. "You know what that Rady Cromwell's went an' done!" she says, blowing her breath between her words and giving me no chance to say a thing before going on. "He's moved that Flary Pringle back down in the holler! Hit's a disgrace, that's what it is! That woman had ort to be run off the ridge!"

It was a time for keeping your mouth shut, so I said nothing. But I couldn't help thinking that in a way it was a pity Rady couldn't marry her. She was stout and a good worker, and she would be a big help to him in the fields. But of course a man with pride couldn't marry up with a woman like that.

I went over in a week or two to see how he was getting along. He'd cleaned the weeds and litter from around the place and had mended up the fences. He'd whitewashed the outbuildings and straightened things up a right smart. Inside, the house was might near as bare as a barn, for there wasn't a stick of Annie's furniture left. I reckon Jubal Moore had got it along with the place and had moved it out. Rady had a cot in a corner of the fireplace room, and he was cooking on the hearth with a few pots and pans he'd got at the dime store. But it was clean, and his cot was made up fresh. Over by the chimney was his old gittar, and in the corner was his guns, and outside the door was the grandson of his old dog, Drum. He was right back down to scratch.

But he wasn't no more licked than he would of been when he was a kid, knowing what he wanted and getting it. He asked for the loan of my mules. "Got to git my tobaccer patch ready," he says, "an' I'm aimin' on puttin' in a right smart corn."

"Use 'em an' welcome," I says, "an' ary other thing I got you need."

"Much obleeged," he says.

We walked out to the gate, it being time for me to go. "You like it here, Rady?"

He bent over and picked up a green twig and commenced stripping it down. When he had it bare he stuck it between his teeth to chew on. "Not rentin'," he says, "but I ain't aimin' on rentin' long. I'll have it back in a couple of years."

He turned and pointed out over the slope. "This fall I'm aimin' on seedin' another pasture over there, an' I'll git me a start of calves. I'm aimin' on raisin' me a nice beef herd come another year."

I followed his finger and then I looked at him. He was looking up the slope, and I allowed he was already seeing, in his mind's eye, his corn standing high, and his tobacco broad and green, and fat calves feeding on a green stand in the new pasture. And it came over me then why I felt so good Rady was home again. It was because he was Rady and not hell nor high water could ever change him or lick him. It gave a man a braver feeling because he was around, and it made you feel like, because he was your friend, you were a little something of the same breed of man.

I hoped him well. "Jist go up with me," I said, opening the gate.

"Can't," he said, "I got the night work to do up. Jist stay on."

But I had my own night work to do up, if Junie hadn't already done it, me being gone overly long already. So I raised a dust up the road. I looked back once and he was still standing at the gate. I waved at him and he waved back at me. Then the turn of the road put the trees between us. But I knew he was still there.